fiona dunbar

tiger-lily

ORCHARD

Thanks to David Stevens for spontaneously analysing my aura,
thus sparking off a *eureka* moment! And for all his insights on the
subject, too. Thanks also to intrepid adventurer Sue McKay for all
the information about potholing, and to Geoff Morgan for being
Welsh. Most of all, big thanks to my editors, Kirsty Skidmore and
Sarah (not Tiger) Lilly, who really helped me sort things out when
I couldn't see the cloth for all the stitches. You are brilliant.

ORCHARD BOOKS
338 Euston Road, London NW1 3BH
Orchard Books Australia
Level 17/207 Kent Street, Sydney NSW 2000

ISBN 978 1 84616 232 9

A paperback original
First published in 2009
Text © Fiona Dunbar 2009
The right of Fiona Dunbar to be identified as the author of this work has been
asserted by her in accordance with the Copyright, Designs and Patents Act, 1988.

A CIP catalogue record for this book is available from the British Library.

5 7 9 10 8 6

Typeset by SX Composing DTP, Rayleigh, Essex
Printed in Great Britain.

The paper and board used in this paperback are natural recyclable products made
from wood grown in sustainable forests. The manufacturing processes conform to
the environmental regulations of the country of origin.

Orchard Books is a division of Hachette Children's Books,
an Hachette UK company.
www.hachette.co.uk

'There was truth and there was untruth, and if you clung to the truth even against the whole world, you were not mad.'

George Orwell, 1984

'Be yourself. No one can ever tell you you're doing it wrong.'

Anon

Contents

A Note From The Author

Adults behave weirdly sometimes. I know – I'm one of them! One of the many weird things you may have noticed about adults is that they tend to get awfully excited about little rectangular pieces of plastic. They go *bonkers* over them.

I hate to say it, but you may well end up doing the same thing. Let me explain: when you grow up, you will almost certainly have a bank account (maybe you already do, but that's different because some adult is in charge of it). Anyway, the bank will then find all sorts of clever ways of removing bits of the money they're storing for you. That's their job. One way they do this is to send you a really shiny plastic rectangle, which they pretend is a Present. They'll even jazz it up with pictures and send a note with it saying, *Congratulations!* so that it really *seems* like a present. DO NOT BE FOOLED. It is really something called a 'credit card': it's designed to make you spend money you haven't got, and will suck the lifeblood from you if you give it half a chance. Some chain stores will do the same sort of thing, and send you a Present called a 'Loyalty Card'. Again, BEWARE.

And that's not all. Sometimes these plastic rectangles are stolen, and this can result in something called 'identity theft'. Imagine that! Someone stealing your identity...

But hey, you don't have to worry about all that just yet. This story, like the two before it, takes place at some point in the future. I deliberately don't say when. But I expect that by the time I'm talking about comes around, those shiny plastic rectangles may well have been replaced with something even craftier, even more dangerous. And the business of stealing people's identities might take on an entirely different form...

Prologue

Rorie had been thinking a lot about witches lately. And monsters, and kings and queens.

She found that by viewing everything that had happened recently in fairy-tale terms, it was easier for her to make sense of it all. And she found it a curiously comforting way of distracting herself from all those horrors; it made it feel almost as if those things were not really happening to her, but to someone else.

Drawing helped, too. Laying it out on the page, she was able to distil things down to their simplest elements:

Evil witch Misty and her EVIL, GREEDY dog, REXCO...

...are keeping prisoners...

...are controlling...

evil child-snatchers witch Irmine and warlock Harris.

...good wizard Laura Silk and good wizard Arran Silk because they don't want them to do their good magic.

...good Queen Nolita, who ruled over Celebrityland until the spell was broken!

...magical faraway land Minimerica ruled by King Max and Queen Lonnie.

Then she realised something was missing from the picture: herself and her little sister, Elsie. What were they – fairies, perhaps? Yes: good fairies whose mission it was to rescue the good wizards Laura and Arran, and bring down the wicked witch Misty and the all-powerful, all-consuming evil monster Rexco.

Hmm, not a bad bedtime story, she thought. 'Once upon a time,' she told Elsie, 'there were two good fairies called Rorie and Elsie, and they were captured by the evil child-snatchers, and held in their palace along with hundreds of other children—'

'Poker Bute Hall!' added Elsie, getting into the game. 'And the evil child-snatchers Harris and Irmine were...turning the kids into statues!'

'That's right. Living statues who couldn't think for themselves, and just did what they were told to do. But the two fairies tricked the evil child-snatchers and got away...'

'Because one of the fairies had a spell on her that made her able to turn into other people. It was the magic sky giant that cast the spell, when he sent—'

'OK, Elsie, don't let's get too carried away...anyway, the two fairies were given refuge by the good Queen Nolita, in Celebrityland—'

'Is Celebrityland good or bad?' asked Elsie, not

sure any more, after all that had happened.

Rorie thought for a moment. 'It's good *and* bad,' she concluded. 'Depends on the celebrity. Anyway, Queen Nolita was good, but she was held under a spell by the wicked witch, Misty.'

'Yeah: a *forgetting* spell,' added Elsie.

'...Which made the queen evil, even though she didn't want to be. So the two fairies ended up having to escape from her as well, and sailed away in search of the good wizards, Laura and Arran Silk—'

'Wizards? Aren't they fairies? I mean, *we're* fairies, and they're our mum and dad, right?'

'Not in the story; "wizards" sounds better – especially because of what they do.'

'I suppose so.'

'Anyway, their search for the good wizards took the two fairies to the magical faraway land of Minimerica, ruled over by King Max and Queen Lonnie, who they thought might be able to help them...until they discovered that they too were part of Misty and Rexco's wicked circle...'

'And all the people in Minimerica were living statues as well...'

'Yes, so the fairies freed them, then figured out how to break the spell that good Queen Nolita was under—'

'And everyone lived happily ever after!'

'Well...'

Elsie had momentarily forgotten that this was their own story they were talking about, and realised her mistake with a flood of sadness. 'Oh, but *then* the fairies still had to find out where the good wizards Laura and Arran were, and rescue them.'

'Yes,' said Rorie quietly. 'That was the hardest challenge of all.'

'But they're such *clever* fairies!' exclaimed Elsie. 'Just look at all the amazing things they've done already!'

'Yes, I suppose that's true,' sighed Rorie. 'But this one...this one is *really* hard...'

Chapter 1
Kethly Merwiden

'You have arrived at your destination,' purred the car confidently. Rorie, heavy-headed, half-opened her eyes; the pewter skies were now pierced here and there with slices of dawn light over the lush green hills.

'Well, whaddaya know,' sighed Nolita, her New York accent tinged with sarcasm as they trundled to a halt. 'It's the middle of nowhere! Again!'

This was the third time the car had made this announcement, and the third time it had been proved wrong.

'I'm sorry, but I did *tell* you I've never been there before,' said Gula, fiddling with the satellite navigation system. 'The trouble is, she's never heard of Kethly Merwiden.'

'*She?* Who's *she*?' snapped Nolita. 'Stop talking about the car as if it's a person.'

'OK! *It!* Whatever!' *Beep, beep, beep*; Gula went on programming.

Nolita rubbed her eyes. 'OK, I'm sorry. But are you *sure* you've got—'

'The name of the place right – yes, I'm sure,' said Gula.

Rorie shifted in the back seat, trying to get comfortable; her neck ached. She glanced over at Elsie. She was sprawled sideways like a discarded doll, open mouth spilling drool, eyes feline slits, open yet closed to the world. It had been a long night.

Nolita sighed again. 'If only we could just call…'

'No,' insisted Gula. 'I told you, it's better that we just show up. I need to speak to Lilith face to face.'

Lilith was Gula's sister, and they hadn't spoken to each other in about six years. How she was going to feel about the four of them just turning up and asking if they could hide away in the commune, Rorie couldn't imagine. But they were desperate. The very fact that they were relying on Gula proved just *how* desperate; neither she nor Elsie had known her more than forty-eight hours, but they had already found her pushy, loud and generally obnoxious. Rorie couldn't help wondering if this behaviour was a hangover from Gula's days as a celebrity, or the result of her disappointment in the world now that she was a Nobody. Still, Nolita had known her for a long time – and by now the girls did at least feel able to trust her...

'Well,' said Nolita. 'So now what?'

'We look for mulberry trees?' suggested Gula. 'That's what "Kethly Merwiden" means, apparently: Mulberry Grove.'

Nolita stared at her blankly. 'Gula, hon, sorry, but you're gonna have to do better than that.'

Elsie woke and stretched. 'Are we there yet?' she drawled.

'Almost, baby!' replied Gula, beaming back at her. Despite her cheerfulness, Rorie could hear the tension in her voice; this was all Gula's idea, and no doubt she was anxious as to whether it would work out.

'Hey, look. A wind turbine,' observed Elsie, gazing up at the hills from her odd angle.

Gula peered. 'There is? Where?'

'Oh, I see it,' said Nolita, pointing. 'Way up there. Could that be...?'

Gula set the satellite image to photographic mode. 'There's no road on the map, but maybe...ah, here,' she said, zooming in. 'That must be it – there's a dirt track. Here we go.'

*

'Well, well, well,' said Lilith, shaking her head slo⟨w⟩ in disbelief. 'It really is you.' She cast her eyes up ⟨and⟩ down. 'Plus about five stone, I'd say.'

Gula shifted awkwardly, trying to ignore the insult. Like her sister, she was heavy-set, but whereas Lilith was solid like a tree trunk, Gula had grown bloated from years of hot fudge sundaes and missed aerobics classes. 'Hi, Lil. *Ahem*, these are my friends, Nolita, Rorie and Elsie.'

Lilith stepped forwards and greeted them in a polite but detached manner. She looked and smelt like someone who had grown in the woods, like a fungus. Her weathered, bare face was handsome, and she wore a nose-ring. Her dry, earth-coloured hair hung in weighty, matted wads down to her hips. She wore odd-shaped clothes in muted colours, which seemed to consist of a long dress, a loose-knit cardigan and a very long scarf – as well as half a dozen other indeterminate, flimsy items. As she shook her hand, Rorie felt the roughness of skin used to hard physical labour; she noticed Elsie's reluctance to touch it.

'Lil, I can explain everything,' said Gula. 'But we've come a long way, and we're very tired—'

'All right. You might as well come in.'

*

The settlement had once been a quarry, Gula had explained, hewn from the Welsh mountainside. Like Lilith, the moss-roofed homes looked as if they had grown there; they were part-cave, with stone-built facades. The look on Nolita's face was one of barely concealed distaste as she picked her way among the clucking chickens in her silver leather high-heeled boots; it couldn't be more removed from the glamorous lifestyle she was used to. For that matter, Rorie could well imagine it was worlds away from the 'Beverly Hills' on Minimerica that Gula had been used to for the past two years – the fake celebrity land that was really a dustbin for has-beens. But neither Nolita nor Gula remarked on anything; life was going to be very different from now on. It would have to be.

Lilith's home was bigger than Rorie had expected, and circular. Light filtered in from above, and low-level seating surrounded the central kitchen area. A short, bearded man, hair hung in loose plaits, emerged from one of several curtained doorways, fastening his long shirt and adjusting his necklaces as he went. He looked like a sweet, overgrown puppy who'd collided with a six-year-old's dressing-up box.

'This is my partner, Bilbo,' said Lilith.

Bilbo greeted each of them with both hands. 'Welcome,' he nodded earnestly.

Elsie stared at his sandals and the rings on his toes.

Lilith noticed. 'At Kethly, we largely ignore mainstream values of clothing choices,' she pointed out. Elsie's face remained clouded.

'Yes,' beamed Bilbo. 'We opt for a fashion of self-determination. Tea?'

'Yes, please,' said Nolita and Gula, and they followed him to the kitchen area.

'I don't understand what they're saying,' Elsie whispered to Rorie as they followed.

'It just means they don't follow any set rules,' Rorie whispered back.

Elsie's eyes widened. 'Oh! Cool.'

'So, Gula,' said Lilith as they sat down. There was frost in her voice. 'How's the *celebrity* world these days?'

Gula's eyes lowered. 'Well, Lil, things have changed—'

'Aah! You don't say!' said Lilith sarcastically, fiddling with her scarf.

'Lil,' said Bilbo, a note of warning in his voice.

Lilith checked herself. 'Go on, Gula.'

'Nolita here is the person who discovered me,'

continued Gula. 'Rorie and Elsie are...well, that's a whole other story. The point is...' Her lower lip began to tremble. 'Oh, Lil, you were right all along! All those stories of yours about the big bad corporate machine, exploiting the people...now I know it's true!' She burst into tears.

Nolita comforted her, patting her on the back. 'Please don't be hard on her,' she told Lilith. 'She's had a terrible shock.'

'She would never listen,' insisted Lilith.

'*Lil*,' repeated Bilbo, touching her tenderly on the shoulder. 'This is interesting...carry on, Gula.'

Gula blew her nose. 'For the past couple of years I've been living in – well, a place I *understood* to be Beverly Hills...' She sighed. 'But...oh, what's the use? It all sounds so silly now!'

'The fake Beverly Hills is part of an island called Minimerica,' Rorie explained. 'It's a floating, man-made island.'

'We discovered it!' added Elsie proudly.

'Elsie!' laughed Rorie. 'You make it sound like we're Victorian explorers, or something!' She turned to Lilith. 'What she means is, we're the ones who exposed the secret.'

Lilith nodded. 'Which was?'

'Well, it *was* a discovery really,' Nolita pitched in. 'Because Minimerica itself was the secret.'

'Yeah,' added Elsie. 'See, nobody knowed about it, 'cause it moved around, and was hidden in this cloud, and—'

'A man-made mist,' Rorie added. 'And there was a satellite deflector...'

'I knew it!' cried Bilbo, clicking his fingers. 'Lil, this is that rumour we were discussing just last night.' He turned back to Nolita and explained. 'We've had snippets of information...we have certain *sources*, you see. There's nothing about this on the newsnet, of course.'

'Well, I haven't exactly had time to look, but...no, I'm not surprised,' sighed Nolita.

'What? Why?' demanded Rorie indignantly. 'You mean that after all we've done, this isn't a major scandal?'

'Because, honey, Rexco are so powerful,' explained Nolita. 'They controlled me, didn't they?'

Suddenly Rorie felt about the size of a flea. She'd been convinced that once this story came out, Rexco, the giant mega-corporation behind Minimerica, would be finished. Had nothing she and Elsie had done amounted to anything?

'It's hard to get a handle on exactly what's going on, though,' said Bilbo. 'Do tell us more.'

'Minimerica was an elaborate exercise in mass deception,' explained Nolita. 'As you apparently realise, Rexco run practically everything at this point. And they've achieved this by infiltrating the minds of staff in their clothing stores, their financial institutions…'

'Their schools,' added Elsie.

'And, as we've seen, in the media,' Nolita concluded. 'Including me. Hey, I was a whole industry all by myself.'

'She was,' sobbed Gula. 'And she was brilliant. Brilliant!'

Lilith's face was blank. Unlike just about everyone Rorie had ever known, Lilith had apparently never even heard of Nolita Newbuck.

'I kind of generated the whole celebrity fashion machine,' Nolita explained.

'She was an inspiration to millions!' added Gula, dabbing away her tears with a handkerchief.

'Yeah, but she din't know about the spider,' Elsie pointed out.

Lilith looked confused. 'The *spider*?'

Nolita pulled down the side of her boot to reveal

a raw, red scar. 'See this? They embedded a chip, here; the wound was hidden by a spider tattoo. I didn't know it, but I was being programmed by Misty, my reflexologist. Every time she massaged my feet, she was able to erase any memory, just like *that*.' Nolita clicked her fingers. 'I lived only in the moment, never looked back. In with the new, out with the old, over and over, faster and faster...'

Lilith exchanged glances with Bilbo as he placed the tea on the table. 'Ah, I get it. And Rexco were the ones supplying all the new fashions, right?'

'Yes.'

'Which,' Lilith continued, 'presumably helped to make these Rexco people ever richer, more powerful...'

'Exactly.'

Lilith frowned. 'I still don't understand what happened to you, Gula. Why were you sent to this island?'

Gula twisted the handkerchief. 'It's where Rexco sent us ex-celebs, when no one was interested in us any more. It's also where they sent their employees for a nice brainwashing holiday every once in a while...'

'*Rexco is kind, Rexco is good, we all love Rexco,*'

25

chanted Lilith, as if reciting a mantra. She seemed quite unsurprised by it all.

'Right, that sort of thing,' said Gula. 'They put stuff into the food, the information system...even the air we breathed! It had us believing we were still great, still adored. Waking up to the realisation that nobody cares any more is pretty hard to take, I can tell you...' Gula blew her nose loudly.

'*We* care, Gula,' said Bilbo earnestly.

Lilith shot him a look; he poured the tea.

'Hey, what about our parents?' cried Elsie, leaping to her feet. 'What's happened to them is much worse!'

'OK, honey, sshh!' soothed Nolita. 'This brings us to why we're here, Lilith. I'm in hiding – Gula told me I'm unlikely to be tracked down here.'

'Well, that's true,' nodded Lilith.

'And part of the reason for that is so that I might help these girls find their parents, Arran and Laura Silk. Now that we know what kind of brainwashing Rexco are capable of, we believe they've done something similar to Arran and Laura, who went missing over three months ago.'

'Really? Have the police been involved?' asked Lilith.

'Yeah: 'Spector Dixon,' Elsie chipped in.

'There's an Inspector Dixon who's been working hard on this right from the start,' Rorie explained.

'Well, yes, but so far he and his team have found nothing at all,' countered Gula, 'let alone anything linking the disappearance to Rexco—'

'Yes, but they *are* behind it. We're sure of that now!' added Rorie. She felt her face grow hot.

'They're very clever,' said Gula. 'Stories *do* circulate, no matter how much Rexco try to control things, but they're already dealing with those rumours you've been hearing. Check this out.'

She produced a memory card from her bag, and inserted it into a dusty old computer. The screen lit up with glowing images of Las Vegas, New York, Hollywood.

Many people are nostalgic for the days of the American Empire, said the voiceover, *and not just Americans. That's one reason why we have created Minimerica – so that everyone can live out their own American Dream!*

'Ugh!' muttered Lilith.

This is just part of Rexco's ongoing commitment to improving people's quality of life, continued the voiceover. *Our long-term research programme has shown that breaks of the kind we offer play an important role in balancing people's lives and warding off depression; this is why we believe in entertaining our employees at our own expense. No other major employer achieves this, and it is why we are proud to say that Rexco are the world's foremost investors in people.*

Lilith stood up abruptly, hitting the pause button. 'Enough. My digestive system needs time to regain its equilibrium.'

Elsie looked to Rorie for a translation. 'She's worried she might throw up,' Rorie whispered.

'You see what we're up against?' said Nolita. 'The slightest whiff of suspicion anywhere, and right away they're turning the whole thing to their advantage, bringing it out into the open and pretending that the only reason Minimerica was being kept secret was because it was a piece of "experimental research".'

'But will they succeed?' asked Lilith. 'What about all those substances you were telling us about, the mind manipulation...how are they going to explain all that?'

'It's possible that they've already destroyed the evidence,' said Nolita. 'We really don't know. And then there's what these girls managed to expose about Misty and the spider tattoos: she did it to others, too – nearly got Gula here. Rorie turned over incriminating film to the police, but we're still waiting for that story to rock the foundations of the Rexco regime. So far, not a word. But whether or not they manage to wriggle out of all this with their reputation intact, you can be sure of one thing; they're mad as hell that this has happened.'

'And we're the ones they're angry with,' added Rorie.

'The bottom line is, Lil, we're scared,' said Gula. 'We believe this whitewash campaign is just one part of their programme of damage limitation.'

'What's the other part?'

'They have us killed.'

Chapter 2
The Incredible Shape-Changing Dress

'You're in luck,' explained Lilith as they brought in their bags. 'Some people moved out of the SLG just last week.'

Gula frowned. 'SLG?'

'Small Living Group...wow, you really don't know anything about communal living, do you?'

Rorie noticed a flicker of irritation on Nolita's face, and wondered how much more of Lilith's superior manner she would take before saying something.

A young couple with a baby appeared. Lilith introduced them. 'This is Grover and Skye...and here's Baby.'

Gula patted the baby on the head. 'Hello, baby.'

'No, the baby's name is River,' corrected Lilith.

'*This* is Baby,' she added, waving at another woman who had entered the room.

'Oh! Hi,' said Rorie.

Baby was followed by her young daughter, Dream. Rorie held out her hand, but instead of shaking it Dream stared at the scar on Rorie's palm and said, 'What's that mark?'

'Oh...nothing,' said Rorie, pulling down her sleeve.

There was an awkward pause. 'Well, *ahem*, and this is John,' said Lilith, as an older man appeared.

'Just "John"?' asked Gula.

'Just John!' grinned John.

'I got everyone up,' said Lilith, 'so as to facilitate a dialogue among the whole group about the changing reality of our living space.'

Nolita cast a glance at Elsie's puzzled face, then said to Lilith, 'To...discuss the possibility of our staying here?'

'That's right,' she said.

'So all of you people live right here, in this one house?' asked Gula.

'Yes. But as I say, some others just moved out.'

They all sat down. Lilith explained the circumstances of the new arrivals to the rest of her housemates, while Dream, who looked about nine years old, stared at Rorie and Elsie. Elsie stared back; Dream had a slightly wild look about her, with bare feet, matted hair and grubby sleeves.

'...I think you'll agree,' concluded Lilith, 'that just because these poor people took the hardest route to reach the same core belief systems as us, it does not mean we should spurn them.'

Rorie noticed Gula and Nolita exchanging glances.

There were nods and murmurs of agreement all round. 'Our enemy's enemy is our friend,' said Grover.

Skye, rocking her baby, agreed. 'I think this would be a very healing environment for them.'

'All right,' said John. 'But we'll need to explain how we do things here.'

'Yes, I was about to do that,' said Lilith.

'Oh, brother!' muttered Elsie under her breath – a little too loud, as it turned out.

Despite herself, Gula burst out laughing.

Lilith's eyes lit up with a black fire. 'Do you mind sharing the joke with the group, Gula?'

'Sorry, Lil, but can we have plain language, please, for us *poor, simple folk* who didn't have the wit to figure out what *you, of course,* knew all along.'

'There's no need to be sarcastic,' retorted Lilith.

'All right, now, he-e-e-ey,' soothed Bilbo, rubbing

Lilith's shoulders. 'One thing we *really want* our newcomers to know is that we're *really good* at conflict resolution, right?'

Lilith took a deep breath, and stood up. 'Right. Well, probably the best thing would be to show you round.'

'Hey, I'd love to come with you, but I've got to go to work,' said Bilbo, rising. He seemed hesitant, like someone about to walk away from a house of cards and worrying it was going to collapse.

'Oh, digging the garden and stuff, huh?' said Gula. 'That's nice.'

Lilith glared at her. '*Actually*, Gula, we run a highly successful business, making recycled household objects and clothing. And I should be working, too.'

'Well, don't let us keep you,' retorted Gula.

Nolita stood up quickly, smiling her diamond-studded smile. 'Thank you, Lilith, you're very kind to let us stay. We'd like to be shown around, but...maybe later? This has been very stressful, and we're all completely bushed.'

'Oh, of *course*,' said Bilbo, joining forces with Nolita in trying to keep the peace. 'We should let them lie down, Lil. Realign their chakras, adapt to their environment.' He beamed. 'That's all it'll take.'

'Yes,' said Lilith tersely. 'I think that may be what's *needed* here. Come on, I'll show you to your rooms.'

When Rorie woke, she couldn't remember where she was at first. Then, taking in the sloping, craggy whitewashed walls and the homespun wall hanging, the words 'Kethly Merwiden' resurfaced in her mind. *Here we are again*, she thought, *somewhere different*. In the space of little more than three months, they had gone from Poker Bute Hall, to Nolita's mansion, to a stolen boat, to Minimerica, back to Nolita's...and now here. Rorie thought about her own bedroom back at home, with its clutter and chaos, its ever-evolving collage of pictures, and her heart ached. That bed was probably still exactly as she'd left it, with the duvet tossed aside...the same pair of socks would still be lying on the floor. And what about her parents' room; would that ever be inhabited again?

And so, as she dozed, Rorie's thoughts turned to Mum and Dad. As was her habit at such times, she found herself replaying, scene after scene, all her happiest memories – especially those from their last couple of days together, fourteen weeks ago. The day before Mum and Dad disappeared, she and Elsie had been treated to a demonstration of the long-awaited secret invention that Dad had been working on for so long. She saw it now, as clearly as if it were yesterday. There stood Dad, down in his basement laboratory, exhausted, but eyes shining with excitement at his breakthrough...

'So-called "Smart" clothing,' said Dad, 'like the thinfat jacket, the heart-monitor vest, clothing that plays music and displays pictures – has become a part of everyday life. But until now, we've had to rely on electronic components woven into textiles, which means limited capabilities and lifespan. So I began to look at completely new ways of making Smart clothes...going back to nature!'

Behind him, screens showed a fish, a cat and a newly hatched butterfly. 'New ways to advance thinfat technology...'

The fish puffed itself into a ball, the cat's fur fluffed up in hostility, and the butterfly's wings became thin and rigid as they filled with blood.

'...And colour-changing technology.' An octopus, a zebrafish and a chameleon appeared on the screens.

'Lols?' called Dad, and Mum emerged in

knee-high black boots and a plain white dress. 'What sort of day is it today?'

'Hmm,' said Mum. 'I'd say it was a RED day...' The dress instantly turned red. Elsie and Rorie gasped in admiration.

Mum beamed. 'With PURPLE POLKA DOTS,' she added: the polka dots appeared. 'No, SMALLER...SMALLER...GOOD.' The pattern on the dress altered according to every verbal instruction.

'Once the dress is programmed,' Dad explained, 'it can be locked in that mode until you decide to change it. There are a hundred and fifty different modes,' – the dress flicked through each of them before their eyes – 'but with further development, it should be possible to have hundreds more!'

'I want one!' cried Elsie.

'It's incredible,' gasped Rorie.

The patterns stopped changing, but Mum remained fixed to the spot, grinning mischievously.

'Hey, don't stop,' pleaded Elsie. 'Do it again!'

But Mum just stood still, the dress fixed in the same pattern.

'Oh, look!' said Rorie, just as Elsie was beginning

to lose patience. 'Did you see that? The dress is—'

'Oh! It's getting longer!' cried Elsie.

Soon the hem of the dress almost reached the floor. 'And...*voila*,' announced Mum. 'It's an evening dress!'

Elsie peered around the back for clues. 'How d'you *do* that?'

'You probably didn't notice,' explained Mum, 'but your dad was sending the dress remote instructions from a device on his wrist. At the moment we can only make it long and short, but with further development you could program the same garment with dozens of different styles!'

'Hmm...the boots are all wrong,' Dad pointed out.

'Oh, of course!' said Mum, inspecting them. 'Silly me!' She clicked her heels together, like Dorothy in *The Wizard of Oz*. Immediately the long boots began to shorten, transforming into low-heeled shoes. Next, the heels grew higher and narrower, until they were a perfect pair of evening shoes.

Elsie got down on her hands and knees. 'Wow! I want some o' them, too!'

'We call them "superbootshoes",' said Mum. She laughed. 'Oh, Arran, it works like a dream now...'

Dad had gone on to demonstrate how useful the technology was for packing luggage, by shrinking clothes to a fraction of their normal size. Rorie had been amazed. She had always known there was something very special about the thing Dad had been obsessively working on for the past several months, but 'works like a dream'? It was beyond her wildest dreams! She had of course asked how the technology worked – but her understanding of the explanation was sketchy. It had to do with DNA, she knew that much. She always remembered Dad posing the question, 'How does a rose remember to become a rose, and not a cauliflower?' – then answering it by explaining how the DNA in every cell of every living thing provided those instructions. The big breakthrough, it seemed, was his discovery of how to wirelessly communicate such instructions to alter once-live cells, like wool no longer attached to a sheep. Rorie still couldn't fathom quite *how*; it had all seemed like magic to her.

'And the beauty of it,' Mum had explained, 'is that it doesn't wear out.' Every time the garment changed, the cells renewed themselves; dirt and sweat particles were just swallowed up, as the program knew they didn't belong there. Magic! A child would no longer outgrow their clothes; laundry would become a thing of the past. With the right development, these ideas would revolutionise the way people lived. 'The planet will heave a massive sigh of relief,' Dad had said...

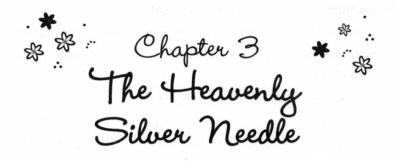

Chapter 3
The Heavenly Silver Needle

Awoken by clap of thunder, Rorie sat bolt upright. She gasped; it was a sound that struck fear in her heart. Elsie, on the other hand, slept on, blissfully unaware.

Restless, Rorie got up and went in search of the bathroom. She heard the rain pelting down outside, accompanied by further grumbles of thunder. On her way back, she peered into the living space, to see if Nolita or Gula were up yet. She saw Lilith, stirring a big pot of something at the stove. There was a delicious smell coming from it that might have been inviting, but Rorie retreated, not wanting to be seen. She found Lilith rather scary.

But Lilith had seen her. 'Hey,' she called warmly. 'Sleep all right?'

Rorie turned round awkwardly. 'Uh, yes...thanks,' she said, twisting her sleeve with her fingers. She took another step back, ready to retreat.

'It's OK,' said Lilith, flashing her a mischievous grin before tipping some chopped herbs into the pot. 'I don't bite.'

Rorie gave a sort of pretend laugh.

'Come, talk to me while I cook. Sit!' She indicated a chair with the knife. She gave her a lingering, amused look. 'You needn't be nervous of me, you know.'

'Oh, I'm not,' Rorie lied, stepping forwards.

'Oh, yes, you are. It's all there, in your aura. I can see.'

'My...aura?'

'No one ever taught you about auras?' asked Lilith, as she pulled out some bowls from a cupboard.

'No. *Auras*, did you say? Not "Auroras"? That's my full name: Aurora.'

'Lovely name,' said Lilith. 'Means dawn.'

'That's right.'

'Not so very different, really. Glowing light appearing on the horizon. Well, you've got an aura of glowing light surrounding you – we all have.'

Rorie frowned. *This is weird*, she thought.

'Just because you can't see it, doesn't mean

it's not there,' said Lilith. 'But you can *learn* to see auras, you know; anyone can. Now, *you*...' she peered, eyes directed slightly above Rorie's head, '...have a child's aura, bright and clear – yet with developing sophistication. Healthy balance of colours. Plenty of red: you're determined – in a good way.' Lilith's eye moved toward Rorie's shoulder. 'Strong presence of orangey-yellow, shows intelligence, good analytical skills...yet there's darkness there, too, a cloudedness. Doubt.'

Rorie looked away, uncomfortable under the scrutiny. 'Well, yes, I suppose...'

'I'm sorry about the conflict between me and Gula. We're just very different,' explained Lilith.

Rorie could see the kindness in her eyes now. She supposed she couldn't really blame Lilith for not getting along with Gula who, she already knew, could be a major pain in the neck.

'But what I'm most sorry about is what happened to your parents,' added Lilith. 'I want you to know you're welcome here. And we want to help you.'

'Thank you,' said Rorie, sliding onto a bar stool close to Lilith. 'Um...could you tell me more about auras? I'm really curious...'

*

The storm quickly retreated; by the time it had roused the rest of them, the clouds were scudding off into the distance, leaving everything glistening in the sunshine. Lilith proposed that they head out for their tour of Kethly Merwiden.

Rorie paused at the front door, scanning the skies anxiously. 'I don't know, Else. Why don't you just go on ahead, and I'll stay here.'

'No way!' said Elsie. 'I'm not going without you.'

Rorie bit her lip, still staring upwards. 'But what if…'

Elsie sighed, and put her hands on her hips. 'The storm's *finished*.'

Rorie pulled herself back inside, and leant against the wall. 'There might be another one.'

'Rorie, you won't get struck by lightning again,' insisted Elsie. 'I promise!'

Rorie laughed nervously. 'Oh, you'll see to it, will you, Elsie? You'll make sure the magic sky giant stays away?' She gazed out again at the retreating storm clouds, unable to help herself as she relived the moment: running away from Poker Bute Hall, carrying their pet chameleon Arthur Clarkson. One careless move, grasping the steel shaft of an umbrella, and *wham!* the heavenly silver needle of electricity had bolted through one hand and out the other, stitching girl and pet together. Fusing them.

Rorie rubbed at the scars on the palms of her hands, as if she were trying to erase them.

Poor Arthur Clarkson had not survived the experience, but it had left Rorie with a lot more than just those scars. It was almost as if the spirit of Arthur Clarkson had entered her; she had become, effectively, a human chameleon. Which meant that if she put on someone else's clothing, she took on their physical appearance. Not *completely*...it was more a kind of merging of identities. But it was very disconcerting, all the same. Then she had discovered something else; she took on not only a person's appearance, but their skills as well. So if the person was a great athlete, Rorie became one, too. If the person knew how to drive a car, sail a boat, fly a plane...well, Rorie could do that as well.

This was not something she shared freely with others. It was her Big Secret.

Elsie knew, of course. And Nolita had found out for herself – but only about the physical changes. And by now, there may be others who knew, too – but Rorie didn't want to think about that.

Lilith and the others emerged, ready for the tour.

Rorie took a deep breath; she really didn't want to look like a wimp. Nor did she especially want to say anything about her accident. All the same, she was nervous. 'Um, will there be somewhere to shelter?' she asked. 'You know, if there's another storm?'

'Oh, don't worry about that,' Lilith assured her. 'No shortage of places; we'll be close to shelter at all times.'

Rorie stepped forwards tentatively. 'OK,' she said at last.

'Mind your step,' Lilith warned Nolita, as they climbed the steep, stony path that ran alongside some vegetable terraces and fruit orchards.

'Serves me right, I guess,' laughed Nolita, as she staggered along in her hopelessly impractical heels. 'Shoulda changed.'

Lilith tossed a couple of freshly picked apples to Rorie and Elsie, and peered at Nolita's boots. 'I hope you don't mind my asking, but do you actually *have* any country clothes?'

'Well...no,' admitted Nolita.

'Thought not. Well, we'll have to see what we can lend you.'

Nolita forced a smile. 'Oh...thanks. I hope you

don't mind *me* asking, but…when did you last go to the hairdresser's? I'm not being rude, I'm just curious. Your hair is so…' She trailed off, unable to find an appropriate adjective.

Lilith let out a sharp, guttural laugh. 'Hairdresser's? You *are* joking?' She eyed Nolita's sleek auburn bob. 'Now, at a guess, I'd say *you* go for at least two hours, once a week. A hundred hours a year…hmm…over a couple of decades, that's nearly a quarter of a year; think of all the *useful* things you could do instead! I neither cut nor wash my hair. Waste of time.'

Nolita cast her eye over Lilith's matted dreadlocks in a way that suggested she thought differently, but she said nothing. 'So what's that big building over there?' she asked, pointing to a large structure at the top of the hill, next to the wind turbine.

'That,' announced Lilith proudly, 'is the factory. Come on, I'll show you.'

Even though they'd hardly covered any distance at all, Gula was becoming breathless. 'Oh, it's OK, Lil, we don't need to see inside or anything.'

'Gula, how can you possibly expect to integrate into our society in any meaningful way, if you don't make yourself open to understanding what we're all about?'

Gula stood still, gasping for breath. Her face was red from the exertion of climbing the hill. 'Hey, it's just a factory, right? A factory's a factory's a factory.'

Nolita leapt in, diamond tooth sparkling. 'Uh, what she means is…sorry, Lilith, but Gula has problems with her legs.'

Lilith looked at Gula's swollen ankles. 'Well, all right, we needn't go far,' she conceded. 'But the factory's right here. And for your information, Gula, there can be a whole world of difference between one factory and another. Good grief, aren't you even *interested* in what we're doing here?'

'I am!' piped up Elsie, crisp white flecks of apple spilling from her mouth.

'Me too,' said Rorie.

'Good. And it may interest you to know, Gula, that you will be working in the factory.'

Gula stopped in her tracks again. 'Hey, who are you kidding?'

Lilith put her hands on her hips. 'What did you think, that you'd just get to hang out, as a non-contributing guest? We *all* work at Kethly Merwiden, Gula, every one of us. We don't use money; our earnings from the business go back into the business.

So: you want something, you work for it. Are you telling me you have other skills we could use? Accountancy? Management? Construction?'

'Oh, Lilith, I'm sure Gula didn't mean—' Nolita attempted, but it was no use.

'No, I did mean!' interrupted Gula. 'This isn't fair – she's just on a power trip. *Have I any other skills? Tuh!* She knows very well how big a star I—'

'*Used* to be, Gula,' retorted Lilith. 'And we've got plenty of good singers here as it is, thank you. At Kethly, song is play, not work.'

'That's it!' snapped Gula. 'I'm not listening to any more of this.' She turned to Nolita, Rorie and Elsie. 'I'm sorry. I thought this might work out, but I was wrong.'

'Oh, Gula...' sighed Nolita.

'When are you ever going to get down off your high horse, Gula?' Lilith called after her sister's retreating figure. 'Oh, you were always so-o-o superior, with your limousines, your fancy designer clothes—'

'Oh, *I'm* superior, am I?' interrupted Gula, spinning around. 'You should hear yourself, with your, "just because these *poor* people only *now* understand the threat from the Big Bad Corporation"...ugh! Is that any way to extend a helping hand? With insults? Oh, and just out of interest,' she went on, 'how *exactly* is it that you knew all along, huh? How did you *know* Rexco were slowly turning the entire population of this country and beyond into mindless drones?'

'I—'

'Admit it, Lilith; all you had was just a bunch of stupid, crackpot theories! Very easy *now*, to be wise with hindsight, isn't it? And what were you doing about it, huh? Besides just hiding yourselves away from it all? These kids have actually made a difference to other people. Come on, girls, we're leaving!' Gula turned on her heel and began marching, bottom wobbling furiously, back down the hill.

'Oh, but I like it here!' wailed Elsie, bursting into tears.

There was a loud honking noise. 'Aargh!' cried Gula. Rorie turned and saw that Gula had nearly walked straight into the path of a small tractor that was emerging from the orchard.

'Watch out!' shouted a male voice.

They all ran down the path. 'Gula, are you all right?' asked Nolita, stumbling over her heels as she went.

'You ought to watch where you're going!' Gula yelled at the tractor driver.

'Well, so should you!' retorted the driver, leaning out. Rorie's jaw fell open. 'Luke? Is that you?'

Chapter 4
Trapped

'Blimey, what the heck are you doing here?' said Luke, stepping down from the tractor.

'We could ask you the same thing!' said Rorie.

Lilith stepped forwards. 'You know each other?'

'Yes – Luke was a groundsman at...this school we went to.' Rorie shivered inwardly as she thought of Poker Bute Hall, run by Uncle Harris and Aunt Irmine. Such a strange, sinister place. She would never forgive Uncle Harris for behaving as if Dad was known to be dead; and the way he had tried to con Great-Grandma into cutting Dad out of her will and leaving her considerable riches to him alone was despicable. Thankfully, Great-Grandma, even at 112 years old, was still as sharp as a pin and could not be duped.

Elsie flung her arms around Luke's legs, which was all she could reach. 'He's our friend!' she cried.

Rorie felt her cheeks flush with pleasure; she too was very glad to see him, and the memory came rushing back of the day when he may just have saved her life, reviving her after she had been struck by lightning...

She cleared her throat. 'When did you leave Poker Bute Hall?'

Luke grinned as he wobbled under the weight of Elsie. 'Not long ago...oh, I'm so glad we're out of there, I can't tell ya! Been wanting to leave for years, but Mum saw it as her mission to mother all the girls in that school. "No one else will do it!" she'd say. I mean, I know she was nurse and everything, but...anyway, I didn't feel I could leave her behind.'

'What, did she leave too?'

'Yeah, she's here. Eventually things got too weird even for her. I finally convinced her that worrying about what was happening to those poor girls was making her ill, and we should, you know, make a fresh start.'

Rorie remembered the secret supply of booze Pat had kept in a milk carton in her fridge in the sick bay; Pat Dry was really not a well woman. 'You mean she's...better now?'

Luke nodded. 'Doesn't touch a drop. "Dry by

name, dry by nature", she likes to joke. Mind you, *chocolate*...now that's a different story.'

'Oh, Luke!' gasped Elsie. 'Can we live with you and Pat?'

'Can you *what*? What are you doing here, anyway? I thought you were staying with that fashion lady...?'

'You mean me?' said Nolita, stepping forward. 'They are, it's just that I'm...kind of, in hiding.'

'We were going to stay with Lilith,' said Elsie, 'but Gula hates her now—'

'You're in hiding?' interrupted Luke. 'How come...who are you hiding from?'

Nolita swept back her hair wearily. 'Well...my bosses. Not so different from your situation in a way; I've had enough. I've paid off my staff; they're probably just now getting the video messages I left for them. I'm done with it all. I just want to help Rorie and Elsie now.'

'Good for you,' said Luke. 'But why are you hiding from them?'

'It's Rexco, Luke.' said Rorie. 'And guess what: they were your boss, too.'

Luke looked perplexed. 'How d'you mean?'

'Look, Poker Bute Hall is run by Tramlawn Schools, right?'

'Right.'

'Well, guess who owns Tramlawn? Rexco.'

'An' it's them who also stole our mum and dad!' added Elsie.

Luke's jaw hung open. 'What?'

'Well, we're only *guessing* that part,' explained Rorie. 'But it's a pretty strong hunch at this point. Rexco are *evil*, Luke. And dangerously powerful.' She glanced at Nolita, as if to ask for permission to explain further: Nolita nodded. So Rorie told Luke all about what Misty had been doing to Nolita, and what she and Elsie discovered on Minimerica. 'It all links up, don't you see? They're taking over every aspect of people's lives. They want us to be like robots, so they can run everything, unchallenged.'

'The corporate Emperors of the World,' Lilith chipped in.

'And what they're doing at Poker Bute Hall is crushing every drop of individuality, right from an early age,' said Rorie. 'You know those "Anger Management Courses" they send the "difficult" ones on?'

Luke bit his lip. 'Oh yeah, I know about them all right. If you must know, I went to that unit – where they were sending the girls. I wrecked it. Then me and

Mum got out. Not running away, you understand; it's just…'

'We're all in the same boat,' concluded Nolita.

'And you've all come to the right place,' added Lilith. 'Together, maybe we can beat the machine – strength in numbers.'

Luke looked thoughtful. 'But we can only do that if we're undetectable.' He turned to Nolita. 'You've disabled the GPS on your car, right?'

Nolita frowned. 'You mean the SatNav? No, should I have?'

'You didn't? Oh boy! You know they could have traced you, don'tcha? It would be easy for them to pick up on your satellite signal.'

Nolita's face turned white. 'Oh my…I forgot about that. We were lost, you see, and I just…'

'And I didn't think of it either,' added Lilith. 'Last thing on my mind, I'm afraid.'

Rorie had been so sleepy, she certainly hadn't thought of it. 'But we didn't *start out* using it…'

'Well, that's something, at least,' said Luke.

Nolita put her hands on her hips. 'OK, just how bad is this?'

'Hard to say,' said Luke. 'I mean, yeah, it's a heck of a lot harder for them to track you if they're not beamed into your system right from the start – as you can imagine, with all them satellite signals coming off other vehicles. But they have their ways, and we'd better do what we can to cover your tracks. Where are you parked?'

'Uh, back there…'

Luke pulled his Shel from his pocket. 'What make and model? Registration?'

Nolita gave him the information. Luke relayed it to his Shel, then snapped it shut.

'OK, look, come with me,' he said, beckoning as he moved on. 'Best not to be out in the open, at least for a while. You never know.'

'What's happening to the car?' asked Nolita, as they all hurried to keep up with Luke's forceful stride.

'Getting a change of ID,' said Luke. 'How long have you been here?'

'Two or three hours.'

Luke sighed. 'OK, well…we'll do what we can. I've sent instructions to swap systems with one of our vans. Then the van'll go out on a delivery. If Rexco are on your tail, that ought to divert them.'

Rorie felt reassured…but not for long. Because a moment later an ominous, low thrumming sound began to fill the air.

Everyone looked up.

'Oh no,' said Nolita, as a helicopter appeared. 'I think it might be too late for that.'

'Quick!' said Luke. 'Follow me.' He took them down a secluded path that led through some shrubbery, back towards Lilith's place.

'You go ahead,' said Lilith. 'I'll go back and...explain to the others what's going on.'

'OK,' said Luke. Pausing at another house nearby, he told the others, 'Stay hidden. I won't be a sec.' In another moment he reappeared carrying a canvas bag, and they continued on their way.

The thrumming grew louder, more defined, like a pounding heart. 'Come *on*, Elsie!' called Rorie, as her sister picked her way delicately among the nettles.

'I don't wanna get stung!' cried Elsie.

'Oh!' gasped Rorie in frustration as she looked down at Elsie's skimpy little skirt. Why did she always have to dress so impractically? 'Here, jump up on my back.'

Phut-phut-phut-phut-phut went the noise, softer and louder by turns as it circled overhead.

'Where we going?' asked Elsie, but Luke was too far ahead to hear above the din.

'I don't know,' said Rorie. 'Look, hold on tight, will

you? Argh! Don't pull my hair!' With a spurt of energy, she rushed forwards to catch up. 'God, Elsie, you're getting heavy,' she panted.

Gula, too, was proving a liability. Rorie could just make out Nolita's voice, complaining: *Look, I know you got problems, but you gotta RUN, Gula!* and Gula, replying, *I don't DO running!*

Up ahead, Luke had stopped.

'Where we going?' repeated Elsie, sliding down off Rorie's back as they joined him.

'There's a cave up there,' said Luke. 'But we have to go out into the open to reach it.' He looked up at the helicopter. 'They're gonna land; that means they have to head back east of here, where it's level...there they go. OK: now!'

They scrambled up a rocky incline to the cave.

'I don't do caves,' complained Gula, as she approached the entrance.

'Gula?' said Nolita.

'Yes?'

'Shut up.' She pulled Gula forwards by the sleeve.

'So we wait here, till they're gone?' Rorie asked Luke.

Luke pulled a torch from his canvas bag. 'Not as simple as that, I'm afraid. Look, your engine was switched off a couple of hours or so ago, right here at Kethly Merwiden. Don't take a Sherlock Holmes to work out that Kethly Merwiden is most likely where you are. If you ask me, they're going to want to do a thorough search.'

Rorie turned hot and cold at the same time. She gulped hard. 'So, uh...what do we do now?'

Luke shone the torch towards the back of the cave. 'Ever been potholing?'

Chapter 5
Rock-Girl

'Sshh!' hissed Luke. 'Not a sound. Remember, if we can hear them, they can probably hear us.'

Rorie, Elsie, Nolita and Gula stood like statues, instinctively clinging to the wall of the tunnel. Helped by light from the torch and from a caving helmet he had produced from the bag, Luke had guided them to the back of the cave. From there, it had been a sharp descent into a pothole. Needless to say, Gula had hampered their progress in getting down there, but it had been easier than Rorie had dared hope. And she was sure the entrance to the pothole was so obscure that no one who didn't know about it could find it. All they had to do was wait until the Rexco people moved on. They listened: above the constant echo of rushing water came the sound of footsteps on gravel in the cave above them. Then voices, surprisingly clear.

'How many caves are there around here, anyway?' came a man's voice.

'Downloading survey now, sir,' said his companion.

At the word 'survey', Rorie exchanged alarmed glances with the others. She pictured in her mind's eye the man standing there looking at his Shel, as a detailed 3D image of the local topography downloaded onto it. Just how detailed would it be? Would it include potholes?

She shivered.

A chilly dampness seeped out of the rock and into her bones. She found herself wishing she could become one with the stone through her contact with it, in the same way that she blended herself with another person when she put on their clothes. If she could only do that, she wouldn't have to breathe. She could just *be*. Rock-girl. Or perhaps tree-girl – a living, growing thing, yet one whose life was wonderfully simple. A tree could stay in exactly the same spot for its entire life, and all anyone asked of it was that it produce leaves, blossom and fruit, which it did as effortlessly as humans grew hair and nails.

Gula whimpered. Rorie's nerves jangled; the woman was a liability, no doubt about it.

'Did you hear something?' came the man's voice from above.

Then, even more chilling, the words: 'Get the dogs down there.'

Rorie's heart leapt. Dogs? This was some real search unit they had here! Which probably meant they'd have already been to Nolita's house and got them to have a good nose around; if the dogs came down here, they were bound to sniff them out.

Luke gestured wildly to them all, the lamp on his helmet sending shafts of light this way and that in the gloom. He guided them down the tunnel, where it narrowed sharply, and disappeared into a crevice between two great slabs of rock. Everyone except Elsie had to stoop as they went along. Rorie had the misfortune to be behind Gula's outsized backside. She noticed how her hands gripped the walls, clinging on for dear life, and wondered how long it would be before she fell, got stuck, or started freaking out.

Luke knows where he's going, Rorie told herself, as the darkness thickened around them. Could this get any narrower?

On they went, the only light-sources now being Luke's helmet and torch. Murky phantoms seemed to dance around the walls as Luke moved around. *How brave Elsie is being!* Rorie thought.

Then came the sound they were dreading: distant barking. Gula whimpered again.

'Sshh!' Nolita hissed back.

Gula paused. The barking drew nearer. *Oh, come on!* thought Rorie. She wanted so badly to push her.

Then, just as Rorie thought she would lose her mind with worry, the narrow space opened out into another cave. Here was the water they'd been hearing; a narrow waterfall, tumbling from high up in the cathedral-like space. Rorie was grateful for its noise, which she hoped was masking the sounds they were making as they trudged through the gravel and silt around the edge of the subterranean pool.

Luke turned to face them and pointed; he seemed to be indicating that they should climb up to the hole that the water was falling from. *No!* thought Rorie. *You must be out of your mind!* But, looking around, she could see no other way out, besides the way they had come.

Gula whimpered and shook her head violently. Luke patiently walked back to her, took her by the arm, and whispered something to her. After what felt like an eternity, he managed to coax her along.

Woof, woof! The barking was more distinct now – though hard to tell how near. That spurred them on; even Gula hurled herself at the wall and began to climb. There were plenty of footholds, so Rorie was relieved to find that the climb was easier than it had initially seemed. Luke scrambled up first, then helped each of them in turn. Poor Nolita was still struggling in her high-heeled boots, but she probably wouldn't have been any better off leaving them behind, and in any case they would have been a dead giveaway. Soaked, Rorie reached the top of the climb to find Gula plugged into the hole like a cork, her legs flailing. Luke braced himself, then gamely placed his hands squarely in the middle of each buttock and gave a shove. A muffled squeal came from inside the tunnel. 'Nolita, can you hear me?' called Luke as loud as he dared to her, as she'd already gone through. 'Can you pull?'

Rorie couldn't really hear, but it seemed as if Nolita was doing all she could at her end. Nothing: Gula was well and truly stuck. The barking came nearer. Rorie guessed the men had found the passageway they had taken. She clung on to the rock, her arms aching. She was soaked to the skin.

'OK, Gula, listen to me,' said Luke. 'You can get through. All you need to do is try to calm down. The tension in your body has made it swell up; you have to relax.'

Relax! Gula? *Oh no*, thought Rorie, *now we're really done for.* The barking grew louder still, reverberating all around them. Luke went on muttering soothing words to Gula, his voice masked by the echoing waterfall. Whether or not Gula could hear, Rorie couldn't tell.

Suddenly, the loudest bark yet prompted Rorie to twist round; she could barely make out a thing, but there seemed to be movement. Then a flash of light from Luke's helmet, and there it was, the glimpse of a beagle; they'd been seen. Crazed barking. At that very moment, Gula's legs shot up the hole: she was through.

Chapter 6
Lilith's Scarf

Back at Lilith's house, Pat Dry was waiting for them.
She fussed around with towels and clean clothes – no
time for any hellos or introductions. 'Oh, my dears,'
she gushed, as she rubbed away at Elsie's head, making
it wobble like a nodding toy. 'Whatever have you been
up to?'

'We were chased through the caves an' tunnels!'
cried Elsie.

'Ooh, you're lucky to have got through in one
piece!' exclaimed Pat. 'My goodness, there was
one lad, I heard, got his leg crushed under—'

'Thank you, Pat, we'd rather not hear about that if
you don't mind,' said Rorie, remembering how Pat
was inclined to share much more information than
necessary about such things.

Gula flopped into a chair, put her feet up and began

fanning herself. 'Oh, I thought I was going to die! Where's Lil?'

'Off out of here with Rorie and Elsie's things,' explained Pat. 'That young'un with the baby, Skye – she was here too, gave her some help. They'll hide your stuff, don't you worry; all we need to do now is hide *you*!'

'Yes, and we'd better hurry up,' said Luke. 'These guys have dogs.'

'Dogs! Oh, my!' gasped Pat. 'Not pit bulls, I hope? Oh, there was one little girl I heard of—'

'No, Mum, they're *beagles*,' interrupted Luke, sparing everyone another gory story. 'And they're on our scent trail. Only reason they're not here yet is, they'll have had to go back the long way around, through the tunnels – beagles can't climb up sheer rockfaces—'

'*I* can't climb up sheer rockfaces!' Gula pitched in.

'You just *did*, Gula,' Elsie pointed out.

Gula's eyes rolled heavenwards. 'Never again. Never!'

'I guess it'll also take the dogs a while to pick up on the scent trail again,' remarked Rorie.

'Yeah, but for all we know, they're onto it by now,' said Luke. 'And one thing you can bet on:

they ain't gonna give up till they've got you. C'mon, you're dry enough; let's get you away in one of our vans.'

'That won't be possible,' said Pat. 'The place is swarming with police. I saw a whole team of cars and vans in the compound, sealing us off – nothing's coming or going.'

'The police?' said Rorie. 'But surely...that doesn't make any sense. If anyone should be in trouble with the police it's Rexco, not us!'

'Did it actually say "police" on the side of the cars?' asked Luke.

'Well no, now you mention it,' said Pat. 'It said "Zedforce".'

'What's Zedforce?' asked Rorie.

'I don't know,' said Luke. 'But whoever they are, I think it's a fair bet they're working on behalf of Rexco. And they've clearly got some muscle.'

'Oh boy, here we go – now they've got their very own secret police,' said Nolita.

There was silence as everyone tried to figure out what to do next.

'All right. I'll talk to them,' declared Nolita at last.

'What?' gasped Gula, pausing in her fanning. 'But—'

'Trust me, Gula. I know what I'm doing. You will present yourself as well.'

'What about us?' asked Elsie.

Nolita thought for a moment, then turned to Luke. 'That factory of yours. Got any strong-smelling chemicals and stuff you use there?'

'Not really,' said Luke. 'Everything's natural. Smelliest place I can think of is the biofuel plant, where we turn our compost into fuel, but...if you're thinking of masking the girls' smell, it ain't going to work...a mate of mine's in the police – the *normal* police, that is – and them dogs, it's like they've got x-ray vision of the snout. They're trained not to be put off, no matter what.'

Rorie's heart sank. She had begun to eye Lilith's scarf, which was draped over the chair in front of her, and to think about disguises. But if they could still *smell* her...

'OK, but all we need to do is buy some time,' said Nolita. 'I think I can deflect this whole situation. If you can just hide the girls temporarily at this biofuel plant...'

'I can take them there,' said Pat. 'But actually *hiding* them won't be easy. I mean, I might find some little nook to squeeze Elsie into, but *Rorie*...that's not so easy...'

But what if my smell changes too? Rorie wondered. It had never occurred to her to think about this before, and she'd never tested the theory, but it seemed logical; after all, everything else about her changed when she put on someone else's clothing, didn't it? Now she remembered something Elsie had once said, which made her think that perhaps the scent did change. Rorie had been in the guise of someone called Geoff, when Elsie had wrinkled up her nose and accused her of having BO. Well, she didn't *normally* have BO. And it wasn't some smelly shirt of Geoff's she'd been wearing; only a hat...

'That's OK,' Rorie said at last. 'You just take Elsie, Pat. I know what to do.'

'But—'

'I mean it,' said Rorie, making eye contact with Nolita, the only person in the room at that moment who might just understand what she was thinking. Please, just go.'

Nolita seemed to understand. 'Trust us,' she told Pat. 'We'll be fine. Go on. But hurry, they're probably out of the caves by now!'

'Right,' said Pat, helping Elsie into an adult shirt, which was like a dress on her. 'Off we go, missy.'

'Be careful!' called Rorie anxiously.

'She'll be OK, don't worry,' said Luke, patting her on the shoulder. 'Right, I'm going outside to be your lookout. The minute I see anything, I'll go like this—' He made a distinctive, trilling call like a blackbird.

Rorie took the scarf and disappeared into the next room to make her transformation in secret. Meanwhile, Nolita began briefing Gula on what to say. Although Nolita knew about Rorie's chameleon changes, it was only the *physical* ones she was aware of. Nobody except Elsie and Rorie herself knew that she could take on knowledge and ability from her subject. As for what Gula would make of her change – well, she would be perplexed, no doubt about that! And not for the first time. But Rorie couldn't worry about that; the important thing was to avoid being caught by Zedforce.

Rorie had no sooner wound the long, lightweight scarf around her neck, than she heard a faint blackbird song, followed by a flurry of activity on the other side of the door. The Zedforce men were about to appear.

Chapter 7
Double Agent

'Well, well, well!' came the man's gravelly voice from the next room, amid much excited barking from the dogs. 'Miss Nolita Newbuck. Found you at last. You *are* Nolita Newbuck?'

'I am,' confirmed Nolita. 'But...you mean *I'm* the one you're looking for? Oh, that's so funny! I thought you were looking for the Silk sisters, the same as I am. What can I do for you?'

Rorie held her breath as she stood by the door, listening. She felt nauseous, though whether from fear or the effect of the transformation, she couldn't tell. It was certainly a familiar sensation; as she watched her hands grow larger and rougher like Lilith's, she thought nervously of how much more powerful these transformations seemed to have become lately.

'Well, we rather thought the girls were with you,

madam,' said the Zedforce man. 'I mean, I don't know why *else* you'd have been running away from us in those caves back there.'

'Running away? Oh, Mr – what did you say your name was?'

'I didn't. It's O'Brien. And this is Miss Gula Wray, is that right?'

'Yes,' came Gula's uncertain voice.

'Well, Mr O'Brien,' said Nolita, laughter in her voice. 'You don't know me very well, do you? It may not have occurred to you, but I'm not generally known as someone who goes plunging into potholes on a regular basis. Neither is Gula. We went down there with Luke, here,' – Rorie concluded that Luke must have followed the men into the room – 'but then I started to get claustrophobic. He had to get me out of there as soon as possible. Isn't that right, Gula?'

'Uh-huh. Freakin' out, she was.'

'I wanted to check whether the girls were in there; apparently it's a popular hiding place for fugitives.'

'Oh, I know,' replied O'Brien. 'But your story is as full of holes as that hillside, Miss Newbuck,' he added stonily.

Oh good grief! thought Rorie, her whole body tensing up as she heard the snufflings of the dogs on the other side of the door. They seemed very interested indeed.

'Number one,' O'Brien went on, 'I don't see how or why you would have concluded that the sisters had come here, of all places—'

'I—'

'Number two, why should I believe you didn't all come here together? We know the girls came to you at your London abode only yesterday. Why would they leave so soon, and by themselves?'

'Mr O'Brien,' said Nolita, 'with respect, if you just give me a chance, I might be able to explain. What you don't know is that Rorie...has this ridiculous crush on Luke...'

Rorie's eyes widened. *What?*

'...I mean, she's quite unhealthily obsessed,' Nolita went on. 'Isn't that right, Luke?'

'Oh! *Yeah*,' came Luke's voice. 'We knew each other at Poker Bute Hall, where I used to work...' He trailed off.

'*And?*'

Luke cleared his throat. 'Right, well...she'd had this accident, see. She'd fallen unconscious and I kind of brought her back round, doing the...'

'Mouth-to-mouth resuscitation?'

'Yeah. And ever since then, she's had this thing for me.'

Rorie felt her face flush with annoyance. How dare he! *No*, she told herself; *I mustn't let it bother me*. He was trying to save her. Let him tell whatever lies were necessary.

'She had "this thing" for you,' said O'Brien sarcastically, 'yet she's been gallivanting around the country for some time, and only now come here?'

'Mr O'Brien,' retorted Nolita, 'nobody has said Rorie and Elsie *did* come here; only that I thought they *might* have. Rorie had stayed in touch with Luke, and we knew he'd moved here. We thought Luke might have hidden the girls from us, but now we know that's not the case. We've done a thorough search; they're nowhere to be found.'

'Oh? And what about the satellite images we have of the four of you together, here at Kethly Merwiden? What about those, eh?'

Rorie thought her chest would burst. They had *satellite images*? Oh, no. Then they were definitely done for. Still the dogs snuffled – but no barks yet.

'I'm afraid that's impossible, Mr O'Brien,' insisted Nolita. 'Why don't you show them to us? Perhaps we can help you identify who you in fact saw?'

'Madam, I cannot do that for confidentiality reasons—'

'Ah! I thought not.'

Rorie closed her eyes and let out a little sigh; Nolita had called his bluff. Well done, Nolita! It wouldn't even have occurred to Rorie that O'Brien had been lying.

'Oh, Luke, there are some documents on a memory file in my car that might help Mr O'Brien. Would you mind getting it for me? You'll find it in the glove compartment.'

'OK,' said Luke.

'Right,' said Mr O'Brien, as Luke left, 'while he's doing that, we'll continue our search, starting with this house.' His voice grew louder. Rorie jumped away from the door and sat on the bed – seconds later it opened and in bolted two excitable beagles, followed by the two grey-suited Zedforce men.

'Oh, hello!' said Rorie, with a rather exaggerated casual air. All the more so because she had to conceal her surprise at finding that, like Lilith, she could now see people's auras – dogs' ones too, for that matter. It was most disconcerting.

The dogs made straight for her, and sniffed around her feet and legs, tails wagging furiously. What did that mean? Did they recognise her smell or not? Rorie felt herself grow clammy. She stood up to greet her visitors.

O'Brien turned his sallow, greasy face to her and scrutinised her features – again, was there recognition or not? It was hard to tell. Rorie studied his aura for clues: murky blues and pinks indicated a dishonest, repressed nature, but recognition? It seemed O'Brien was not yet sure about that himself. Rorie cursed the fact that she hadn't had a chance to consult a mirror, but if the look of surprise on Gula's face was anything to go by, she must have changed considerably.

The seconds crawled by. O'Brien's breath smelt of bad drains. A dribble of sweat rolled down the back of Rorie's neck. *Snuffle, snuffle* went the dogs...

Finally, O'Brien spoke: 'And who is this, then?'

Rorie heaved an inward sigh of relief.

'Oh, this is...' Nolita trailed off.

Rorie pitched in, but almost said 'Lilith' by mistake. 'Li...Livia,' she corrected quickly. She stretched her arms. 'Sorry, I'm a bit sleepy; just been taking a nap.'

Gula was still gazing at her, almost cross-eyed in disbelief. She looked away, shook her head slightly, then looked again. The greens and yellows of her aura were clouded by grey: uncertainty. But to Rorie's relief, she said nothing, and O'Brien hadn't noticed her reaction.

Now Rorie turned her attention to Nolita's aura. In sharp contrast to Gula's, it was full of strong, clear red and orange, which Rorie-as-Lilith knew indicated a powerful, energetic character.

Nolita stepped close to O'Brien and fixed her sharp green gaze on him. Her voice took on a deep, intimate tone. 'Mr O'Brien, I sent Luke away on a false pretence, because there's something secret I need to discuss with you – something that Gula and Livia here are in on. You see, the famed Nolita Newbuck has gone missing for a very good reason: I feel I can be more use to Rexco in their present crisis as an undercover agent.'

There were flashes of deep indigo in Nolita's aura, a sign that she was relying on feminine intuition; after all, she didn't know for sure that Zedforce were working for Rexco, or that O'Brien would admit that they had a crisis on their hands.

But his response told them all they needed to know. He raised an eyebrow. 'Do you now?'

'I've *always* been a hundred per cent behind Rexco, Mr O'Brien,' Nolita went on, clearly encouraged by his reaction, 'and always will be.'

O'Brien's eyes narrowed. 'Why should I believe you?'

'Because you have no choice,' replied Nolita. 'The girls are not here, Mr O'Brien. If I was aiding and abetting those two little criminals, you'd have every right to haul me in for questioning. But I'm not – you have nothing on me at all. For heaven's sake, I've been searching for them for exactly the same reason you have!' She moved even closer to him. '*Use* me, Mr O'Brien.'

O'Brien eyed her up, nodding slowly. 'All right, Miss Newbuck. What exactly do you propose?'

'You want the Silk sisters, right?' said Nolita.

O'Brien punched the wall with a loud *thud!* that made Rorie jump. 'You *bet* I do!' he barked, baring his teeth in a grotesque, thin-lipped grimace.

'Then leave it to me,' said Nolita. 'I know how to lure them back. For one thing, I can use Luke as…bait, if you like. And while I'm about it, I can spy on these Kethly Merwiden people. They'd love to see Rexco tumble from power, you know. And they think I've renounced it all, dropped out, because that's what I want them to think!'

Rorie was impressed with Nolita's act – it was very convincing.

O'Brien stroked his chin thoughtfully. 'Hmm, that would be good, too...'

'I'll get those girls for you, Mr O'Brien,' said Nolita. 'You can count on it.'

Chapter 8
The Silk Farm

'Ah, Rorie, there you are,' said Nolita, as Rorie entered the room.

'Hi.' Rorie gave a little wave to everyone, and quietly seated herself beside Elsie.

An emergency house meeting had been called following the Zedforce incident, but Rorie had had to remain shut away in her room for some time, waiting for her appearance to return to normal. It had taken *so* long…

'I've just been telling everyone about my discussion with O'Brien,' Nolita told her. 'Rorie's been pretty traumatised by events,' she added, by way of explanation to the rest of the group.

At the same time, Rorie felt Elsie's finger dig into her side. 'S'all right,' Elsie whispered. 'She din't tell about you-know-what.'

Rorie knew she was talking about her Big Secret: how she transformed. 'Good!' she hissed back. She eyed Gula. Unfortunately, there had been no avoiding telling *her*, after what she had witnessed. Rorie just hoped she could be trusted not to tell anyone else. And at least, like Nolita, she still didn't know about her ability to take on other people's skills...

'So whose side *are* you on?' John, the senior member of the group, challenged Nolita gruffly.

Nolita blinked at him. 'I'm on your side, of course.'

'Well, how do we know that? You tell us one thing, Zedforce another...you used to be part of the Rexco machine—'

'*Used* to be!' cried Nolita. 'Listen, I told you what they did to me. Every time I was reprogrammed, the slate was wiped clean; even people I'd been extremely close to were erased from my memory.'

'Even us!' added Elsie.

'Right,' went on Nolita. 'What kind of zombie would I have to be to want to remain part of an organisation that did that to me – and to God knows how many other people as well?'

'It's all right, John,' Lilith assured him. 'She's telling the truth; I can see it in her aura.'

Rorie, to whom everything looked rather

disappointingly dull and flat now that she was no longer seeing people's auras herself, was at least reassured to hear this. It wasn't that she didn't believe Nolita; it was just that her act with O'Brien had been so convincing. And Nolita had been pretty unreliable in the past...but then that was *before*. Poor Nolita had had no control over that.

'And let there be no doubt about it,' Nolita went on, 'if I hadn't made this negotiation with O'Brien, you can bet that Kethly Merwiden would still be under surveillance.'

'If you hadn't been here, they wouldn't have come in the first place!' retorted John. 'Even with those Zedforce vehicles gone, this is still a major risk for us.'

'All right, John,' said Bilbo. 'I'm sure we can work this out somehow. Maybe Nolita can show us she's on our side – do some investigating for us.'

'That's another thing!' growled John. 'What's she going to tell Zedforce when they start pressing her for information?'

Grover and Skye nodded in unison. 'He has a point, Bilbo,' Grover said.

'Why don't you let me worry about that,' suggested Nolita. 'And yes, Bilbo, the whole reason I'm here is to work against Rexco; of course I'll do whatever I can.

Or rather, *we* will – Rorie, Elsie, Gula and me. We're a team.'

'And the number one task is to find out what happened to our parents,' said Rorie.

'About that,' said Bilbo, clearing his throat. 'We were wondering, Lil and I...how do you know... I mean, it could be that—'

'How do we know they're still alive?' interrupted Rorie. 'Is that what you're trying to say? Well, we don't. All we know is that they had an appointment with Rexco the day they disappeared.'

'Yeah, an' we think they're being used as inventor-slaves,' added Elsie. 'You know, 'cause they're really brilliant and everything, an' so Rexco get them to do their evil inventing for them or else they kill them, and—'

'All right, Elsie,' said Rorie, silencing her. She turned to Bilbo. 'It's just that after what we've seen them do to Nolita, and to the people of Minimerica—'

'And to the Poker Bute Hall girls,' Elsie pointed out, recalling what had happened after their friend Moll had been sent away on an 'Anger Management' course.

'Right,' said Rorie. 'Well, it wouldn't be unlike Rexco to, I don't know, *use* Mum and Dad somehow, rather than just...you know, the other thing.' She couldn't bring herself to say the words 'kill them'.

'But we have no idea where Rexco would have taken them. All we know is that they never showed up for the meeting they had scheduled at the Rexco base in Shenham, just outside London. But Rexco is global – by now, Mum and Dad could be in New York, or Shanghai, or Kuala Lumpur for all we know!'

'I think our starting point has to be, we go undercover, infiltrate their system,' suggested Nolita. 'So we need to access their database; only then can we hope to narrow our search.'

Bilbo and Lilith exchanged glances. 'Well,' said Lilith, 'there's somewhere near here you might try.'

Rorie felt her ears prick up. 'Really?'

'It's a new silk farm development, right on the borders of Kethly,' said Bilbo. 'We think it might be Rexco-related.'

Nolita gazed at him intently. 'You *think*? Why?'

'Because it's on land that we owned, which wasn't even for sale. But we were forced into selling. I happen to know that this is a typical Rexco tactic. Also, did you know there's been a fierce price war in the garment industry over the cost of silk?'

'Hey, I'm at the "demand" end of the industry – or

rather, I *was*,' said Nolita. 'I left the "supply" side to the other guys.'

'Well, it's pretty brutal, let me tell you,' said Bilbo. 'And here's why: it's all down to those little caterpillars munching on mulberry leaves and making themselves silk cocoons.'

'Yeah, just so that humans can kill them and keep the silk to make dresses from,' added Lilith.

Elsie's eyes were like marbles. 'Is that *really* what happens?'

'Yes,' said Bilbo. 'Because even with all the technology we have, humans have never been able to produce a synthetic version that's anywhere near as good. They can't even develop a breed of silkworm that will eat something else besides white mulberry leaves – or, for that matter, generate a faster-growing mulberry. And believe me, they've tried. Meanwhile, demand for silk just grows and grows; producers can't keep up. That's where that land comes in: it's all white mulberry groves.'

'Hold on,' said Nolita. 'You say you *think* Rexco's behind the buyout. Don't you know? Surely the company name was on the contract?'

'They didn't use the name "Rexco" – the name was De Lusse.'

Rorie looked at Nolita. 'Have you heard of them?'

Nolita shook her head. 'I'm not sure,' she said. 'I've been rebooted so many times, I don't know what's what. But I can look it up,' she added, pulling out her Shel. Her face fell. 'Ah. Rexco have blocked me: I no longer have access to their files. Shoulda guessed they'd do that.' She stared at her Shel for a moment. 'But...they can't get rid of all the data that's already on here. Let me see...' She punched a few buttons, and everybody waited.

'Ah, here,' said Nolita at last. She held it out for them to see. In a 'Rexco Monthly Bulletin' from nearly two years ago was exactly what they were looking for, under the heading 'Acquisitions': 'Silk textiles company, De Lusse'.

Elsie extracted her pyjama bottoms from the ramshackle pile of belongings hurriedly returned from their hiding place. 'I can't believe that's how they make silk,' she remarked. 'It's so cruel! I'm never wearing silk again.'

'Oh, they're only little caterpillars,' said Rorie. 'And I'm sure they don't suffer. They probably just go to sleep and don't wake up again...hang on, why are we even talking about this? I'm a bit more concerned about what Rexco are doing to human beings, to be honest! Hurry up and get into bed, Else. I need to get back and discuss plans with the others.'

'What plans?'

'About the silk farm...don't worry, I'll fill you in; just get some sleep.'

'Not tired.'

'Else, it's *late*, come on.'

'First you gotta tell me a story.'

'Oh, *Else*...'

'Come on, I'll start. Once upon a time there were two good fairies, Rorie and Elsie, and—'

'OK, OK, just a quick one,' said Rorie. 'But first you've got to get under the covers.'

Elsie quickly jumped under the patchwork quilt. 'They're a funny bunch, aren't they, these Kettly Mermaid people.'

'Kethly Merwiden,' corrected Rorie.

'I like Kettly Mermaid better,' declared Elsie.

'Anyway, what do you mean, "funny"?'

'Mud in their hair! And men in skirts! Weird.'

'Elsie! Have you forgotten everything Mum and Dad used to tell us? About being yourself, and who cares what other people think?'

'No, but—'

'What about the tiger-lily story? Have you forgotten that?'

'No! Course I haven't. But that's different.'

'No it isn't, Elsie.' Rorie settled herself on the bed. 'All right. Since we're doing a story, we'll have that one. To remind you.' She took a deep breath. Would she be able to tell one of Mum's made-up stories without bursting into tears? 'OK. Once upon a time...' And as Rorie embarked on the story, the image of Mum sitting on her own bed at home, when she herself was Elsie's age, filled her mind. She could picture her, tired, yet with eyes alight...

'Once upon a time, there was a rich and powerful king,' said Mum, tucking her legs up underneath her on the bed, and leaning against the wall. 'He had a magnificent, dazzling white palace, surrounded by beautiful gardens where every single bloom was a perfect, spotless white. The blossom was white. The lilies were white. The roses were purest, cleanest white. They were the king's pride and joy, and he had a whole team of fairies to keep those flowers scrubbed clean at all times. At dawn they polished the dew from the petals; at noon, they freshened them up with fairy dust to prevent them from turning brown in the sun; at dusk, they polished them again to keep them gleaming brightly.'

Young Rorie rested her head on the pillow, picturing the lovely garden in her mind's eye. Little two-year-old Elsie was in her toddler's bed nearby, sucking contentedly on her thumb.

'Now, the king doted on his daughter, the princess,' Mum continued. 'And she, in turn, adored animals. So the king collected the most exquisite horses, birds and big cats from all around the world, and they were much admired by all who visited them. But the princess didn't care for them, because they too were all white. "Can't I have pink flamingos, or green crocodiles, or red pandas?" she pleaded.'

'Blue monkeez!' suggested little Elsie wetly over her thumb.

Rorie tutted. 'Don't be silly, Elsie, there aren't any blue monkeys.'

'The princess *might* have asked for blue monkeys, for all I know,' said Mum diplomatically. 'Anyway, the king refused. "Everything we own is perfectly white," he said. "It would spoil things to have something gaudy like that."

'But the princess was used to having her own way. So she decided to enlist the help of the fairies. "I want you to paint these ones," she said, indicating two dazzling white horses, "with a gorgeous pattern of black stripes, so they look like zebras."

"Certainly, Your Royal Highness," said the fairies.

"And these perfect white cockatoos," the princess instructed further, "I want you to paint red, yellow and blue like parrots. And this pair of big white cats, I want you to paint with gold and black stripes, like tigers."'

'An' de monkeez—' put in Elsie.

'Sshh, Elsie!' snapped Rorie.

'And so,' Mum continued, 'the fairies went about colouring the animals and birds with their magical fairy paint. Soon the princess had a wonderful collection of rainbow-hued creatures.'

'But the king was furious,' said Rorie, eagerly anticipating the next part of the story.

'Yes,' said Mum, 'and he ordered that the fairies wash all the paint off again. But the animals had come to like their beautiful new colouring, and weren't happy about this at all. They roared and whinnied and squawked at the fairies; they bucked and swished and flapped them away, and chased them back to the flower garden. The poor fairies tumbled through the air, spilling colour everywhere, which landed in great splodges on the flowers, making zebra-roses, parrot-tulips and tiger-lilies. They began to clean up, and were just finished with the zebra-roses, when the king arrived, now even more enraged. The parrot-tulips, afraid, flew away to freedom, but the tiger-lilies remained, defiant. And before the fairies had a chance to explain what had happened, the king began swatting them angrily with his royal fly-swatter.'

'Which is *very* painful for a fairy,' Rorie chipped in.

'Yes, very painful indeed,' added Mum. 'But then an extraordinary thing happened. The tiger-lilies were furious with the king for the way he was treating the fairies, and what was more, they *liked* their new colours, just as much as the animals did. Strong on their sturdy stalks, they wound themselves around his ankles and shook him furiously this way and that, then tossed him across the lawn. The king was flabbergasted! And as soon as he was able to get to his feet, he ran away to the safety of the palace.'

*

Rorie paused in her own telling of the story at this point, suddenly struck by how like her own chameleon changes these floral transformations were. The tulips, clothed as parrots, behaving like parrots. The lilies, clothed as tigers, behaving like tigers. 'This is where I always used to ask Mum how the flowers were able to do those things.'

'Me too,' said Elsie.

'But now I find it makes more sense to me than ever. Remember how Mum used to explain it? "Nobody expects flowers to behave in that way," she'd say. "But just because it's not expected, doesn't mean it's impossible."'

Elsie joined in reciting this last sentence. 'And then,' she added, 'the tiger-lilies were the only coloured flowers in the garden.'

'*Until,*' continued Rorie, 'the other flowers looked and said, "We want colour too!" And so the fairies added pinks to the roses, reds to the poppies, and violet and lavender to the violets and lavender. The king didn't dare interfere, and the princess was delighted. The garden was now a riot of colour, but it would never have happened if the tiger-lilies hadn't stood up for their right to be different.'

Chapter 9
Maggie's Overall

A high wall surrounded the mulberry groves, topped by electric fencing. Beyond the groves was a large white building emblazoned with the logo of De Lusse. At exactly 5.28 pm, Luke deposited Rorie and Nolita at its entrance. 'Well, good luck,' he said. 'In two minutes' time, they'll all be streaming out. I'll be right here.'

'Thanks,' said Rorie nervously, as she stepped out. On the side of the van was a very convincing rendering of the De Lusse logo.

Together, she and Nolita stepped up towards the gate with their clipboards. Nolita smoothed back her brown hair and adjusted her frumpy, brown-framed spectacles. 'You're sure I'm not recognisable?'

Rorie surveyed the grey skirt and blue blouse that Nolita had got from Pat – old Poker Bute Hall clothes, which had undergone some emergency tailoring. 'Nolita, I promise. You look *really dull.*'

'Thanks.'

''Specially without that diamond in your tooth; that would have been a dead giveaway.' Nolita had been able to cover up the diamond-studded tooth with some help from the one and only Kethly Merwiden dentist.

'And my *ex-cent*?' said Nolita, sounding like an English actor from a 1930s movie.

'Well...you could tone down the poshness a bit. Oh look, here they come!'

'All right. Now remember, you needn't say anything; leave the talking to me.'

'OK.'

The uniformed workers streamed through the gate. Nolita approached them with her clipboard. 'Hi...we're doing an employee satisfact...hi, we've been hired by De Lusse to...thank you...hi...'

Rorie was right: Nolita really was invisible today. And nobody seemed to care about the 'employee satisfaction survey' she was pretending to carry out. Then, at last, a young woman with curly blonde hair paused momentarily. Nolita pounced. 'Good afternoon!' she said brightly, in her cut-glass English accent. 'I wonder if you'd be interested in our employee *setisfection* survey...?'

Rorie nudged her discreetly, a reminder not to overdo the accent.

The young woman frowned as she slowly computed the long, posh-sounding words. 'Ooh-er, well, um...'

'What's your name?'

'It's, er, Maggie...'

'Well, Maggie, how would you like a free day off work?'

Maggie brightened. 'What – a whole day? Oh, goowon, then!'

Some of Maggie's colleagues overheard. 'Day off work?' they echoed, huddling around.

Nolita held up a hand. 'Sorry, it's just one in-depth questionnaire per farm – thank you...thank you!'

The workers moaned and shuffled away.

'So what do I have to do?' asked Maggie.

'Well,' said Nolita, adjusting her glasses. 'You just have to answer a few questions...it only takes about half an hour.'

'Half an hour!'

'But you get to stay home tomorrow!' Nolita squinted up at the sky. 'Only...*I say*, it looks like rain.'

Rorie nudged her again discreetly.

'I tell you what,' proposed Nolita, as if she'd just thought of it. 'We're prepared to do this in the comfort of your own home, if you wish. We could run you there in the van.'

'Ooh, ta very much! I usually take the bus.'

Rorie exchanged a satisfied grin with Nolita as they followed Maggie to the van; they had their girl.

'What's Maggie done, then, sent in her sister?' joshed a young man the next morning at the entrance to the farm building.

'I don't know who Maggie is,' muttered Rorie-as-Maggie in her newly high-pitched voice, keeping her head down. 'I'm just a temp.'

Quickly scanning her ID card, careful to keep its picture concealed, she pocketed it and hurried along. It was, of course, Maggie's card; it had been in the pocket of her overall, which Rorie had successfully 'borrowed' after Maggie had taken it off when she arrived home.

'Ah, you're having us on!' said the young man, shoving himself forward in the crowd. 'You're Maggie's better-looking sister, aren't you? Here, what you doing Saturday night?'

'I'm out – wi' me *boyfriend*,' retorted Rorie, hurrying along.

'He-hey, better luck next time, mate!' said the young man's friend, slapping him on the back.

Rorie tucked her lightened hair into her plastic cap and headed to her station. She knew something of what awaited her from the answers the real Maggie had given to Nolita's questions yesterday, and also of course from the information the 'Maggie' part of her brain was now telling her. All the same, there were some things she was not prepared for, and what hit her first was the smell. Now that she thought about it, she supposed she ought to have realised the place would be smelly; it was a farm, after all. But apart from saying that the air conditioning could sometimes be better, Maggie hadn't remarked on it, and it had not occurred to Rorie that *silkworms* would cause such a stink. She'd never seen any before, but they sounded so sweet and non-stinky, somehow. But the place had an unpleasantly sour, yeasty smell.

The next shock she had was the sight of the creatures. After acquiring the overall, Rorie had gone back to Kethly Merwiden and learnt what she could from the net about silk farms, so she might know what to expect. What she expected, then, was trays of mulberry leaves covered with ravenous 'worms' – caterpillars, really – whitish creatures the size of a finger. She expected beds of brush-like thatch covered in the white cocoons the silkworms made for themselves when they were ready to pupate, and baths of boiling water into which the cocoons were plunged to kill off the worm inside and thus prevent them from eating through the precious silk when they were ready to emerge.

But the De Lusse farm was different.

Yes, there were all of these things, but the difference was the scale: these creatures were *huge*. De Lusse – Rexco – had apparently 'improved' on nature and created a species of super-silkworm. They may not have succeeded in getting them to be less fussy about their diet, but they had certainly managed to make them bigger. Rorie found herself gagging as she walked – purposefully, she hoped – to her workstation. Giant caterpillars the size of human babies chomped through piles of leaves – which themselves looked unusually large. Even above the chirpy piped pop music, she could hear the wet smacking noises of their mouthparts. The creatures lumbered over each other in their feeding troughs, spiky forelegs waggling as they raised up their little round, beige heads. These heads looked like noses beneath the monstrous fake black 'eyes' staring out from the raised humps on their backs. The effect was horrific, but all the other workers just went about their business as if all this were normal. Which, of course, it was – for them.

Rorie kept going. She found her way to the harvesting quarter, guided by the 'Maggie' part of her brain. Here she dutifully began easing cocoons the size of overstuffed pillows off the branches of bamboo they clung to. The cocoons were then placed onto a conveyor belt leading to the vats of boiling water. A hissing noise came from that quarter, which might have been gases escaping from the cocoons, or might have been the squeals of the dying pupae; Rorie didn't like to speculate as to which it was. She kept her head down and did her best to avoid any further interaction with her colleagues, while still tugging gently on the big soft egg-like things and sending the creatures inside them to their doom. Soon – not yet – she would find some pretext to go to the supervisor's office.

Dream was beginning to get on Elsie's nerves. It had always been clearly understood among her friends that *Elsie* was the one who played the princess in dress-up games. But Dream had just gone right ahead and started being the princess.

'Look, you *can't* be the princess, OK?' insisted

Elsie, not in the least intimidated by the fact that Dream stood a good head and shoulders above her.

'Why not?'

'Because!'

'Because what?'

'Oh-kaay,' replied Elsie, hands on hips. '*Because* you're all stinky an' mussed up. *Princesses – aren't –* stinky an' mussed up.' She felt a twinge of guilt as she said this, remembering the tiger-lily story, about being different and everything – but found she couldn't help herself.

'I am *not* stinky,' retorted Dream.

'Are too!'

'Am not!

'Are—'

'Hey, hey! Enough already with the fighting, I'm napping here!' called Gula, who was supposed to be supervising the two of them, after Dream had been allowed to take time off lessons and keep Elsie company. Instead, Gula was flat out on the day bed, face creased from the cushions. 'Why don'tcha just…go play in your room or somethin', gimme a little peace and quiet. But remember to stay inside, OK? You got to stay outta sight, Elsie. Now go on, scram!'

But Elsie hadn't actually noticed before that Gula was snoozing, and now that this had been drawn to her attention, the idea entered her head that she could sneak outside. There was nothing to do inside anyway, and it no longer worried her that O'Brien and his colleague had returned to grill Nolita some more; he wasn't in view, and she was bored.

So the two girls wandered out, unseen. However, they did not stop their bickering.

'Your mum's fat,' said Dream, chucking a pebble at the chickens and watching them disperse, clucking.

'*She's* not my mum!' retorted Elsie, throwing some stones of her own. 'My mum's beautiful.' She felt her chin quiver.

'What, Nolita?' said Dream, throwing herself in spinning circles, matted hair flying. '*She's* too skinny.'

'Not her! Don't you know anything?'

'Well, who is your mum, then?'

Elsie folded her arms and turned away. 'Not telling.'

Dream gazed over at O'Brien's purple and silver Zedforce car parked nearby. 'Those guys are taking a long time with Nolita. My mum says they're "the devil in-car-net".'

'What's that s'posed to mean?' asked Elsie over her shoulder.

Dream thrust her face close to Elsie's, eyes widened for dramatic effect. 'It means they're evil, and they have a net in the car for catching people, and once they've got you? You're done for!'

'That's not true!'

Dream threw herself into a cartwheel. 'Ha! You wait and see!'

'NOT TRUE!' shouted Elsie. Then she ran down to the house where Nolita was being questioned, her head swimming with images of her being caught up in a huge net and driven away. She had no idea what she would do if that *were* to happen...but she knew she couldn't just sit idly by and do nothing.

As she drew closer, she crept quietly up to a window, where she could hear the voices coming from inside.

'...been seen in the Manchester area,' Nolita was saying. 'These are the pictures. I understand there's another school like Poker Bute Hall up there?'

'There is, as a matter of fact,' said a man's voice – Elsie guessed it was O'Brien's.

'Well, I think you'd better investigate this as soon as possible, Mr O'Brien,' Nolita replied. 'The Silk sisters seem intent on breaking down the power of Rexco all by themselves...you gotta admire them, in a way.'

'What do you *mean* by that, Miss Newbuck?' O'Brien challenged gruffly.

Nolita was not intimidated by his tone; on the contrary, she was defiant. 'What I *mean*, sir, is that these two young girls are one step ahead of you the whole time!'

Elsie listened for a response, but there was nothing for a moment. 'Manchester, you say, hmm?' came O'Brien's voice at last, quieter.

'I still have a lot of loyal contacts, Mr O'Brien,' said Nolita. 'They wouldn't let me down.'

Elsie leant against the cool, mossy wall and smiled to herself: Nolita seemed to be winning. Satisfied that there was unlikely to be an in-car-net situation any time soon, she moved away. But where to? She *wasn't* going to go back to Gula, and she *didn't* want to play with Dream. Luke and Pat were working; so were Lilith and Bilbo. And in any case, she hadn't wanted to stay home and play – not when there was a big mystery to be solved. Why did people insist on treating her as if she was too small to play an important part? She'd show them.

Chapter 10
Blue Lips

Rorie didn't like being Maggie one little bit. It wasn't just that the job was hateful – although it certainly was. She could still see and smell the silkworms from where she was, and even at a distance they were repulsive. She remembered the time she and Elsie had come across a dead bird on the pavement in the sweltering heat of summer, and a writhing mass of maggots was feasting on its remains. The farm reminded her of a giant version of that. She could only be grateful that at least these creatures weren't chomping their way through rotting carcasses. But although the beasts were repulsive, the fact that others like them were being murdered in their cocoons at the other end of the hall was no less appalling to contemplate...

But none of this was the worst of it. Rorie was beginning to realise that Maggie had chronic breathing problems. It felt as if steel bands were tightening around her chest, making every breath a strain. She remembered an asthmatic classmate from way back in her normal life – which felt like a million years ago now – who got breathless very easily, and always had to carry an inhaler around with her. Was it asthma that Rorie was experiencing now? If so, why should the disease have such a powerful effect on her, when she was still fifty per cent herself? But then the transformations had become increasingly powerful and all-consuming – and it seemed to take longer than ever for her to return to normal. She patted the pockets one more time in search of an inhaler – even though she knew there was nothing there.

I'm never doing this again, Rorie told herself, but she soldiered on, breath rasping as she plucked the cocoons from their branches. Then it occurred to her that there was at least one upside to this situation: she had a pretext to go to the supervisor's office. Surely he would have access to medication? She hoped and prayed he did. She deposited one last cocoon onto the conveyor belt, wiped her hands on her overall, and went over to his office.

'Can I help you?' said the young man, glancing up from his screen.

'I, uh...' Rorie paused, coughing. Her breath rattled its way painfully up her windpipe. 'I...left my inhaler at home...*ahem!* 'Ave you got any?'

'Inhalers? Oh. Um...well, we don't usually—'

'Oh please, I'd be ever so grateful...I got it bad!'

'And none of your colleagues can help?'

Rorie shook her head.

The young man stood up. 'Well, I...hmm. Let me ask around the office. Here, have a seat.' He gestured towards a nearby chair.

Rorie knew she would have to act quickly – which was especially challenging, given the current condition of her lungs. Instead of taking the seat, she wandered behind the desk, then turned and cast a glance in the direction of the open doorway – no one had a view of her through it at this moment, and the blinds on the window next to it were closed. Still wheezing painfully, she concentrated all her energy on the task at hand. Touching the screen brought the electronic desktop to life. After surveying it for a moment, she hit the file marked 'Personnel'. This was subdivided into a list of regions – first, she would look to see if Mum and Dad were listed locally. She tapped 'Swansea': up came a list of staff, the 'S' part of which she scoured as fast as she could. Nobody by the name of Silk. But then, what was she thinking? This was not Minimerica! When she had looked for her parents' names on the database there, it hadn't for a moment occurred to her that the name would have been changed – there would have been no need, since the place was so secret. But here, it would be crazy for them not to! She felt her chest tighten even more; never before had she wanted so badly for someone to return and not to return at the same time! She forced herself to be calm; she could not afford to make the asthma worse. *Think, think!* What other name might they use?

In spite of her efforts to remain calm, spots were now appearing before her eyes. Catching sight of her Rorie-Maggie face in a stainless-steel paperweight, she was shocked: her skin was the shade of porridge, her eyes looked sunken, and her lips were turning blue. She needed help, and she needed it now.

What other name? *Stemphior* popped into her head. Dad's middle name, after the father he never knew. That was really unusual! Find that, and…oh, how her chest hurt, how her breath rattled! Find that, and surely she'd have her clue.

Stemphior.

She checked it: nothing. But she had yet to check the other regions...she tapped 'London', and searched first for Silk – nothing – then Stemphior...

Yes! Two: one male, one female. Her heart skipped a beat; her lungs contracted further...the supervisor would be back any moment now, but she needed to – she needed to check...she searched for images of Mr and Mrs Stemphior, but there were none. There was just one other thing she could look at – the date they joined. And that clinched it: March 10th, 20—. The day after they had disappeared.

Chapter 11
Orchids

'Thank God you're here,' gasped Rorie-as-Maggie, as she got in and slammed the car door.

'Sorry I'm a little late,' said Nolita, as they hurriedly drove off from their rendezvous point, a little way away from De Lusse. 'I was beginning to wonder if I'd make it at all. Those Zedforce guys came back, gave me the third degree.' She peered at Rorie. 'Hey, are you OK? You look kind of pale.'

'You should have seen me before,' wheezed Rorie. 'I've got to get out of this overall – I'm suffering from Maggie's asthma.'

Nolita looked shocked. 'You're…what?'

Suddenly Rorie remembered that Nolita still wasn't aware of the extent of the changes she experienced. She wasn't *supposed* to know, and for good reason; it was a secret only Elsie was allowed in on. It was only because of a mishap that Nolita even knew about Rorie's ability to change her *appearance*...still, this was only a physical change, so she should be able to explain it away. 'Oh...yes, when I "become" someone else, I...take on their diseases as well,' Rorie explained breathlessly. 'Sorry, I didn't think of it. I borrowed...an inhaler, but I haven't used it for a couple of hours now...not sure it was strong enough anyway.'

'Oh, you poor thing!' said Nolita. 'Let's get you back as soon as possible. But, uh...did you get any information?'

'Yes! At least I think so...I'll tell you more later.'

'Of course. You just concentrate on breathing, hon.'

Rorie wriggled out of the overall the instant they were out of sight of the farm gates. She expected the pain to start easing right away, but it didn't; still her lungs were clamped in steel. She closed her eyes and tried to teach herself how to breathe. In, out, in, out...oh, *why* was it still such hard work?

At Kethly, no sooner had they got out of the car than Gula lumbered towards them, distraught. 'You got Elsie with you?'

Nolita slammed the car door. 'What do you mean? She's meant to be with you!'

Gula looked stricken. 'Oh dear...'

Nolita grabbed her by the arm. 'Gula! Where is she?'

'I don't know! I mean, she and Dream were playing, I just nodded off for a bit—'

'You did what?'

'Hey! I was exhausted, OK? They were just playing happily, there wasn't any problem—'

'Only now you don't know where she is! What about Dream? What does she say?'

Rorie was seeing spots before her eyes again. Gula was muttering something about Dream, but sounds were turning foggy under the hissing in Rorie's ears. She slid down the side of the car, chest tightening even more...

There were the words, *What's the matter with her?* Then hands under her armpits, and she was lifted up...

'Keep breathing, Rorie,' said the voice. 'That's it.'

There was something clamped to her face. Cool, sweet air was filling her airways, and the pain in her chest was easing. The figure in front of her gradually came into focus. Pat! Luke's mum; good old Pat. 'There you go, Rorie, that's it, you're doing great.'

'What happened?' Gula's voice.

'Poor thing fainted,' said Pat. 'Must have been the

shock. Wheezy, too, my word! Never knew she was asthmatic. I've given her some drops – Kethly's own remedy.'

'Oh, the poor girl!' said Gula.

'Yes, well, she was pretty stressed out,' retorted Nolita. 'Kind of upset that you *lost her sister*.'

'Never mind now, dear,' said Pat. 'Elsie's been found.'

Rorie pulled the oxygen mask away. 'She has?'

'Yes…she was seen by one of the workers in the apple orchard. Seems she was after finding you! Ah, but she's a one, that Elsie. Mind of her own, and no mistake.'

Rorie could only assume that she was by now fully transformed back to her usual appearance; certainly her lungs seemed to be functioning normally at last. But, just as with the Lilith transformation, it had taken too long! And she had felt so strongly taken over by Maggie that it scared her. There was now no doubting it at all: this transformation was more dominant than the last, which in turn had been more dominant than the one before that, and so on. 'Rorie' was being slowly eroded away each time. She could have suffocated!

Never again, she told herself.

'You just rest now,' said Pat. 'Best leave her alone

for a bit,' she told the others. 'She'll be fine.'

Rorie did feel very tired; the transformations tended to have that effect. She felt herself drifting off...

She was in class at Poker Bute Hall, the awful boarding school run by her uncle and aunt. It was an IS lesson – Information Storage – presided over by Miss Pretty, a hook-nosed lady with a disconcerting squint. Bent silently over her work, Rorie was frantically trying to remember something important. Her eye wandered to the girl next to her, Moll. She had a pale face and dark hair woven into lots of little braids and decorated with trinkets. Moll caught her eye and winked at her. She leant over and whispered, 'Miss Pretty's not looking too pretty today, is she?'

Rorie glanced back at the teacher, and watched in horror as she grew paler and more bloated. So bloated in fact, that she burst out of her clothes, white rolls of flesh oozing forth. Her neck thickened out and her head shrank down until the squashy, pneumatic collar all but consumed it. Finally her face transformed, and she was nothing more than a big, wobbly, disgusting silkworm. She was talking to the class, gesticulating with her tiny stumpy forelegs, but the only sound that was coming out was muffled moans.

Now Rorie looked around, and saw that all the pupils except for Moll were silkworms too. She wanted to scream, but she couldn't. She reached out for Moll. 'We've got to get out of here!'

'Told you there was something weird about this place, didn't I?' said Moll. She seemed completely unsurprised by what was going on around her.

'That's why we've got to get away!' Rorie wanted to cry, but she was mute, immobilised.

Moll just shook her head. 'It's too late...' And now she, too, sank down into the expanding rolls of her neck...

'Aargh!'

'Rorie, wake up,' Pat was saying, shaking her. 'Wake up, dear, you're having a bad dream.'

'Guh!' gasped Rorie. 'Oh, it was so horrible! And Moll...oh, *poor* Moll!'

'There, there, dear, don't you worry yourself now,' said Pat, hugging her. 'Oh, you have been through the mill, haven't you?'

Rorie sat up and took a sip of water. Although she was relieved to find it was just a dream, it had left her with an awful, heavy feeling. 'Pat?'

'Yes, dear?'

'I need to get in touch with someone – someone at Poker Bute Hall.'

'Oh, now, Rorie, don't you think you—'

'Oh, please help me! That dream just now, it reminded me...please, I want to see if I can do something. I feel really bad about what happened.'

Pat put her hands on her hips. 'This is your friend Moll?'

'Yes. You see, they—'

'I know,' said Pat. 'The "anger management" courses; I gather Luke told you about what he did to that unit. Ah, and she was a lovely girl, Moll. So bright, so...well, so *different*.'

'Exactly,' said Rorie. 'And then they went and bleached her out like everyone else.'

'And, like you, I bet she'd never have been sent to Poker Bute Hall by her real mother...you know she was fostered?'

'Yes, she mentioned it.'

'This is really odd, now I think of it,' said Pat. 'You know, *her* mum went missing too...'

'My God, really? Oh, Pat, do you see what's going on here? It wasn't until I went to Minimerica—'

'Mini-whatty?'

'Never mind, I'll tell you later...the point is, I know

now what's really going on. I mean, of course, right now I just want to get Mum and Dad back. But I'm going to help Moll too, any way I can.'

Pat shook her head slowly. 'How do you think you're going to do that, love? You saw how she was when they were finished with her; all shining eyes and a passion for Information Storage.'

'I know, but...look, it might not do much good, but is it possible I could just talk to her?'

'Oh, no way! You know Poker Bute Hall – all contact is strictly vetted. But...I tell you what: Luke's got a friend, Vijay – he's the IT man there, you know, does all the computer stuff...'

'Yes?'

'Well, I suppose we could send *him* something to pass on; that way it would get directly into Moll's hands, bypassing the system. Though like I say, I don't see how you're going to get through to her.'

Rorie was undeterred. 'Brilliant! OK, can I have some paper?'

Rorie made several attempts to write something that might penetrate Moll's pristine, freshly bleached brain, but nothing seemed to be right. Then, several screwed-up balls of paper later, she hit on what to do. She went back to Lilith's, where she found her backpack and got out Moll's necklace. She paused for a moment. This item could be very useful; it had already enabled her to make a spectacular escape, thanks to Moll's codebreaking skills, which Rorie acquired when she wore it...

No. She mustn't think like that; this was the one thing that might just trigger something in Moll's brain about her former self. Rorie took the necklace – a strange, orchid-shaped pendant – and wrapped it carefully in tissue paper. Then she wrote a note:

Dear Moll,
You don't remember, but you made this necklace. You gave it to my sister, Elsie. You told her you were both like orchids; rare, exotic. But then Poker Bute Hall sent you away, and you were never the same again. They're part of a huge organisation that's doing this to everyone. You can help change that. We can work together. Call me...

Rorie put Nolita's Shel number, and gave her name. After a moment's thought, she found a picture of

herself and Elsie and put that in too, for good measure.
Then she finished with:

It's time for the Orchids and the Tiger-lilies to rise up.

Chapter 12
Excess Baggage

Nolita stood up and tapped her glass. 'All right everybody, listen up – we got ourselves a plan. We get this right, and we stand a chance of blowing apart the whole Rexco machine!'

There were loud cheers and table-rappings from the whole assembled house group.

Nolita pointed to the screen she had set up, displaying portraits of Rorie and Elsie's parents. 'Oh, and incidentally – *John* – you'll be pleased to know that I fed O'Brien a series of bogus leads earlier today. Concerning the whereabouts of Rorie and Elsie, as well as the goings-on here at Kethly...'

There were loud murmurings.

'Yeah, we're in Manchester, apparently!' cried Elsie, unable to resist showing off what she'd overheard.

'Elsie!' scolded Nolita. 'You were supposed to

be…oh!' She shook her head and continued. 'Anyway, the point is, that ought to keep them quiet for a while. Incidentally, just in case any of you are still in doubt as to how important it is that we pursue this, let me show you the latest "update" on the Misty investigation I received from O'Brien earlier today.' Next to the two portraits, a short piece of newsnet film began to play, showing first a newscaster:

'*Allegations of gross misconduct against the fashion maven Nolita Newbuck's personal healer and therapist, Misty Grey, were dropped today after it emerged that a film purporting to show Ms Grey implanting faded celebrities with microchips, as a means of controlling their minds, was an elaborate hoax—*'

Rorie stood up and gasped. 'What?'

'Sshh!' hissed the others.

Now the screen showed a young woman being led away in handcuffs by officers, while the voiceover continued: '…*use of lookalikes. The trial is set to take place within the next few days. Ms Grey has been released. Meanwhile, Nolita Newbuck, who recently collapsed from exhaustion, is said to be recovering well—*'

'Who *is* that woman?' demanded Rorie. '*That film's* the hoax!'

'They're pretending *she's* the one who took those shots of Misty?' asked Elsie.

'Yes, Elsie,' said Rorie. 'And it's outrageous!'

'Exactly, of course it is,' said Nolita, amid much murmuring from everyone else. 'And those are Zedforce officers, by the way. It goes on...oh, no, I'll spare you. The story got out that this was all connected to Rexco, but they've got a spokesman saying there's a massive smear campaign being carried out against the corporation, etc, etc... *This* is why what we're doing here is so important.' She banged on the table. 'All right: to business!'

Everyone quietened down. An air of simmering outrage lingered.

'OK, let me summarise what we know so far,' Nolita went on. 'Arran and Laura Silk went missing fourteen weeks ago, on the day they were due to meet with some people at a Rexco base in Shenham, just outside London. We now have more reason than ever to suppose they are still alive because, thanks to some clever undercover work from Rorie, we know that De Lusse – which, of course, we now know to be linked to Rexco – have a record of a man and a woman at the Shenham base, under the name of Stemphior – Mr Silk's middle name. Which is, I think we all agree – even by Kethly Merwiden standards – a pretty unusual name! And they are also recorded as having been there since the day after Mr and Mrs Silk's disappearance.

'Now—' Nolita leant forwards, the table light illuminating her green eyes brightly. 'If these are indeed Rorie and Elsie's parents – and frankly it's hard to see how they could be anyone else,' – there were murmurings of agreement around the table – 'not only do we stand a chance of rescuing them, but...we expose what Rexco have done to the Silks, and we got a bombshell on our hands!'

Again, the excitement was palpable; cheers rang round the room.

Only Elsie was less than thrilled. She already knew she was not part of the plan, and was not happy about it at all. 'Well, *I* could—' she began, but she was drowned out.

'What they *have* done to Mr and Mrs Silk, of course, remains unclear,' Nolita went on. 'But we know that Rexco are capable of manipulating people's minds in all sorts of ways. Now this,' – she held up a tiny metallic object between her thumb and forefinger – 'is a tracking device. Thanks to Luke for having it removed from the GPS system in one of your

Kethly Merwiden vans. Rorie, you are to keep this safely on you at all times. All right?'

Rorie took a deep breath. 'Yes.'

'Having already successfully infiltrated the De Lusse factory,' Nolita continued, 'Rorie absolutely insists that she is the person to do it again. She will return to the factory, with a view to sneaking into the back of a Rexco truck destined for Shenham; this way, she will get beyond the guarded perimeter of the base. I have promised her all the support and protection we can offer. Nevertheless, I think we all agree that she is remarkably brave.'

Amid the applause and murmurings of agreement, Rorie gazed at her hands. She still couldn't quite believe that she had actually proposed to put on Maggie's overall, having vowed she never would again. But the more the group had deliberated about ways to infiltrate the Shenham plant, the more she had realised, with a sinking heart, that she was the only one for the job. What choice did she have? No one else had her powers of disguise. And if this was her one chance to save Mum and Dad, she had to do it. Besides, this time she was prepared; in her pocket, she clutched a small phial of the Kethly Merwiden asthma remedy. She would test it again before she went to bed.

Elsie sat in the corner, pouting throughout the applause. Why did Rorie always have to get all the glory? Because her name rhymed with it? It certainly wasn't because she was cleverer or braver than Elsie. OK, so she could change like a chameleon, but so what? Elsie was a much better actress. No, Rorie was just *older*. Well, how clever was that? *Anyone* could be old; you just had to stick around long enough. Elsie used to think that if she crammed in a few extra birthday celebrations, she'd eventually overtake Rorie in age. But now she knew she would *always* be five years younger than her sister…and on this occasion, the one to be left behind with a babysitter, Pat. How could they do this to her on such an important occasion? She was needed!

'…With the aid of the tracking device,' Nolita continued, 'Luke, Gula and I will be able to follow Rorie out to Shenham – but at a distance of a couple of kilometres, so as not to be detected. Of course, we also know the precise location of the base. At this point we don't know exactly how Rorie will gain access to the buildings once the truck is parked inside the perimeter, but at least we'll be able to keep track of her. She'll also have a Shel on her, with an alarm button set up. Anything goes wrong, we will force our way in. The crucial thing is for Rorie to locate this Mr and Mrs Stemphior, and discover if they are her parents. She'll have the use of this,' – Nolita held up another device, a decorative black brooch – 'a camouflaged movie camera, kindly loaned by Gula. We're going to expose these people for who they really are!'

Further cheers.

Elsie sloped off to her room. There was no way she was not going to be involved in this...

The first people to arrive at the silk farm were always the deliverymen. Rorie knew this because Maggie's boyfriend was one of them. And they came *early*; the sun was still low in the sky. This time Rorie came alone, on foot; it took no more than a few minutes to reach the De Lusse gates via a shortcut on the other side of the Kethly Merwiden orchards. Of course, she would have fitted in more if she were in a deliveryman guise, but the Maggie overall would just have to do. In any case, there were one or two women working in deliveries, and they were dressed the same as Rorie. And, importantly, they carried *bags*; the men didn't. So the bag Rorie clutched was not conspicuous.

And she needed that bag.

It contained her ever-growing arsenal of

transformation kit – which, despite her growing anxiety over these changes, she nevertheless felt safer with, since every item had at one time or another got Rorie out of some extremely hazardous situations. The kit consisted of a couple of accessories, plus fabrics from a range of clothing belonging to different people that she had collected over time – and now included a piece of Lilith's scarf. It was a raggedy old thing anyway; Rorie was sure Lilith wouldn't even notice.

Little swatches of fabric was all she had room for: to carry whole garments would have required a small suitcase. So the night before she had carried out an experiment with one of the items: a pair of trainers she'd stolen from Nikki Deeds – a star athlete at Poker Bute Hall who had turned out to be a wicked accomplice to Uncle Harris. Rorie had taken the linings out, placed them inside her own shoes and, bracing herself for the pain of the transformation, put them on.

Gazing in the mirror, Rorie had watched with a strange mix of satisfaction and revulsion as her hair lightened, her face changed shape. Satisfaction, because the experiment had apparently worked; revulsion, because aside from the pain and anxiety associated with the transformations these days, it made Rorie feel nauseous just 'being' the evil Perfect of Poker Bute

Hall. But she *was* able to do multiple cartwheels and back-flips, and that was so exhilarating it almost compensated for the icky feeling. So she had gone about slicing a waistcoat-shaped section out of Aunt Irmine's jacket (useful for driving a car, and great for 'ageing up') and cutting off a long, thin piece of Lilith's scarf. The other items – the school cravat that had belonged to the brilliant computer geek, Leesa Gates, and the pendant made with real cloned Elvis Presley hair – were small enough to take as they were. Even though the latter one was only good for being Elvis – of limited usefulness, however entertaining – Rorie simply had to hang onto it. What she no longer had, of course, was Moll's necklace; she hoped she wouldn't need to do any codebreaking. Rorie wondered if Moll had received the necklace and her note yet – and what, if anything, she was going to do about it...

Outside the De Lusse gates, the damp of the night was lifting from the ground, forming a flattening mist. A woman and two men were puffing on cigarettes as Rorie arrived.

'Here, is that Sean's girlfriend?' she heard one of them say.

'Surely not, it's too early,' said the woman. Then she called out, 'Maggie?'

Rorie kept going, pretending not to hear. She could hear them muttering, *Well, who is it, then? – I dunno – Is Sean here?*

Good question; Sean might arrive at any moment. Maggie herself should be arriving later, along with the rest of the silk-machine workers, and without an overall. Rorie would certainly have to be away by then! For now, she made herself look busy with an e-notepad, supervising the trolleybots as they wheeled their way back and forth between the loading bay and the trucks. This gave her the chance to survey the backs of the trucks, where their route numbers were displayed, and search for the one marked KS–04; the one going to Shenham. After her detective work locating Mum and Dad, this had been a very straightforward piece of information for Rorie to find on the supervisor's computer.

'Psst!' came a voice.

Oh no, not again! thought Rorie. She kept her head down, pretending not to hear, and carried on.

'Psst, *Rorie!*'

At this, Rorie turned. There, perched just inside the loading bay, wrapped in loose silk, sat Elsie. 'How on earth did you get here?'

'Sshh! I crept out after you,' said Elsie. 'Nobody saw.

And I'm coming with you. Just show me where to go.'

'You are no way—'

'I am!'

Rorie glanced around. What could she do? It was clear Elsie wasn't going to leave her alone, so she may as well go along with it; not to do so would make things even trickier. And now – while the others were still having their cigarette break – was the perfect moment. All she had to do was locate the right truck. Forcing down the bubble of anger that was rising in her and threatening to tighten her chest, she moved quickly along the backs of the trucks – yes, here it was! She beckoned frantically to Elsie, who promptly clambered down from the loading bay. In a moment, they were both well hidden among the bales of silk, ready for their journey to Shenham.

Chapter 13
Nasty Fairground Ride

'How the flippin'eck did you get out again?' hissed
Rorie-as-Maggie, when at last the truck was making its
noisy, bumpy way to Shenham. Irritated by the
Maggie-ness of her voice, she focused on her inner
Rorie, adding, 'My God, they must have been watching
you like a hawk after what happened yesterday!'

'Yeah, they were...till the Zedforce people came.'

'Zedforce? Again?'

'Oh yeah, only much more of them this time. I got
away just when everyone was in a flap about all the
Zedforce cars arriving. It was easy! Oh, and hey,
I borrowed this.' She held up a Shel.

'Elsie!'

'Well, I'll need it. Oh, by the way, I don't

think the others will be coming.'

'What?'

'This time Zedforce are putting up barriers and stuff. I saw them just as I was leaving. Hey, lucky I got out, isn't it!'

'*Lucky?* Elsie, we can't do this without the others!'

'We *are* doing it without the others.'

Rorie pulled out her Shel and switched it on. There was a message from Nolita:

ABANDON PROJECT. Come back now.

Rorie scrunched her eyes shut and threw her head back. 'Oh, I don't believe it! What is the matter with you, Elsie? You *knew*, and you didn't say anything!'

'Because we have to do this.'

'*We?* May I remind you that *you're* not supposed to be here? You could mess this whole thing up!'

'"This whole thing"?' echoed Elsie. 'So "this whole thing" is happening, then?'

'It's...oh, Elsie, you are impossible!' Rorie rolled her eyes. But furious though she was, she had to admit that, having got this far, they had to go through with the plan. What else could they do? They'd hardly be able to do any investigating if they were stranded along with everyone else at Kethly Merwiden.

They sat in silence for a moment. Rorie took the

tracking device out of her pocket and tossed it away. 'Well, I guess I won't be needing that any more. Oh, I'm worried about them all back there now. What made Zedforce come back?'

'Maybe they didn't believe the stuff Nolita told them,' suggested Elsie.

Rorie chewed her lip. 'But what are they going to do? They can't isolate them for ever.'

'They might shut them down.'

'But they can't do that – can they?'

Elsie shrugged.

'They're going to wonder where "Livia" is,' Rorie added.

'Who's Livia?'

'She's a made-up person I was pretending to be, when they came before and you were hiding.'

'They can just say she's out. You know, visiting rellies or something.'

Rorie shook her head. 'But she'd have to come back some time! Oh well, I can't worry about that. Right now I just have to hope I can still find Mum and Dad, and stay alive while I'm about it.'

'Ahem. *We*,' corrected Elsie.

'*You* are staying out of sight at all times,' warned Rorie, wagging a finger. 'D'you hear?'

This stop was longer than a traffic-light stop. The vehicle fell silent and still; with leaping heart, Rorie realised they had arrived. She quickly put Maggie's overall back on, having given herself a rest from the guise for the past three hours or so.

Elsie, who'd been dozing, sat bolt upright. 'Are we—'

'Sshh!' hissed Rorie. 'No engine noise now; *quiet.*'

They had a plan. Or at least, they thought they did. But no sooner had the back of the truck opened than something unexpected happened: there was a loud hum, and they felt themselves being raised up and tipped forwards. Then the container part of the truck began to vibrate quite fiercely; its contents were being shaken out! Desperately, the girls felt around for something, anything, to grab hold of. Hooks – there were at least hooks, though Elsie had some difficulty reaching them. Rorie hoisted her up, which meant that Elsie's legs were left dangling. The two of them clung on for all they were worth as the container jolted them around. Rorie felt as if she were on a particularly nasty fairground ride, made all the more unpleasant by the fact that she was simultaneously morphing into Maggie. Meanwhile, the bales of silk were tumbling out; once they were all gone, there would be nothing to hide behind. It occurred to Rorie that they might grab onto a bale each, and allow themselves to be thrown out – but no: they were sure to be seen that way! She had to admit to herself that neither option looked terribly promising.

The shuddering stopped, and the container lowered itself again. Rorie and Elsie flattened themselves on the floor as soon as they could. A split second later, a man peered briefly inside. Then, lazily satisfied in the way of someone never called on for exacting judgments, he disappeared, and the automatic door began to lower itself again.

Now! They had no choice but to get out; if they were seen now, there was nothing they could do about it. They scrabbled to the door and slithered out, falling to the ground just as it closed.

It was at that moment that they realised they weren't on the ground at all, but on a conveyor belt. Now they were in darkness, trundling down a low tunnel. They still had no idea whether they'd been seen; it had all happened so fast.

'What's gonna happen now?' asked Elsie.

'How do I know?' hissed Rorie-as-Maggie. She felt in her pocket for the bottle of asthma drops, and gripped it tightly. Oh, but this space was *small*. Dark, closing in on her, pressing the air from her lungs...the awful realisation dawned on Rorie that as well as the asthma, Maggie suffered from claustrophobia. Rorie had only been able to cope with a journey crammed inside a laden truck *because she'd taken Maggie's overall off*. That was not an option now. And the claustrophobia, she knew, would soon trigger an asthma attack. Already gasping, she took a swig from the tiny bottle of medicine and prayed this particular journey would soon be over.

It was. The conveyor belt carried them out into a huge, brightly lit space; for a moment Rorie was gripped by a different sort of panic, for being so suddenly exposed. Wondering whether Maggie was afraid of wide open spaces as well as enclosed ones, she soon realised that at least they needn't worry about being seen; they had emerged onto a narrow gallery, high above the factory floor. She slipped off the conveyor belt; Elsie did likewise.

They were in.

Chapter 14
Mr and Mrs Stemphior

The sense of expectation was overwhelming. It felt for Rorie as if her whole life had been building up to this very moment. Having Mum and Dad for twelve years, then losing them. Running away from Poker Bute Hall – and, once her suspicions were raised, from Nolita as well. All her detective work on Minimerica, and at the De Lusse silk farm. Outwitting the sinister Misty, who had been controlling Nolita. Even being out in a storm that fateful night, when the heavenly silver needle had stitched together human and chameleon: so much of what she had achieved since would not have been possible without the extraordinary powers of disguise bestowed on her that night.

All of it, leading up to this moment. Here, at last, would be the reward for all her efforts. Mr and Mrs 'Stemphior' were right here, in this building! And they just *had* to be Mum and Dad: everything pointed to it. In her excitement, Rorie reached for Elsie's hand and gave it a squeeze.

Then she caught sight of the foreman patrolling up and down the factory floor – and worse, the surveillance cameras. Suddenly, Rorie felt like a tightrope walker with no safety net. And without Nolita and Luke close by, ready to intervene, they were completely, utterly alone in all this. They could not afford to put a foot wrong. Oh, curse Elsie for tagging along! Rorie wished she didn't have her to worry about, on top of everything else.

'D32.'

'What?' hissed Elsie.

'That,' Rorie whispered, 'is our clue to finding Mr and Mrs Stemphior. Though what 'D32' actually is, I have no idea. I just know it's the number I saw alongside those two names on the computer at the silk farm.'

'Oh.'

An image formed in Rorie's head of Mum and Dad behind the bars of a prison cell, number D32. Could it really be that there were dungeons lurking somewhere in this building? It was bizarre to contemplate, but how else to explain Mum and Dad's apparent presence?

Rorie remained crouched behind the conveyor belt while she tried to figure out what to do next. From here she could track its progress down to the level of the machines – vast contraptions, she supposed for weaving fabric. Way down at floor level were digital controls, attended by workers; Rorie was relieved to see that they had on the same overalls as she wore. Good: as long as she went about in a purposeful manner, she could at least hope to be effectively invisible.

'We going down then?' whispered Elsie.

'No!' hissed Rorie. 'At least, *you're* not.'

'But—'

Rorie clamped a hand over Elsie's mouth. She knew she would have to concoct some sort of mission for her; Elsie wouldn't settle for less.

'OK, Else,' she said at last, removing her hand. 'See that door there?'

'What, the emergency exit?'

'Yes. Now, I need you to go out there, because I've got an important job for you. But listen: *you've got to stay hidden at all times*. Do you understand? Otherwise you'll be caught.'

Elsie narrowed her eyes suspiciously. 'Hey, are you trying to get rid of me?'

'No, like I said, you need to get outside,

because…because I need you to keep an eye on the place from there, and alert me if you see anything interesting. You've got that Shel. Believe me, it's very important that you do this.'

Elsie didn't look convinced.

'You'll be doing *Nolita's* job for her,' Rorie added.

Elsie thought for a moment. 'OK,' she said at last.

It was a grudging response, but Rorie knew it was the words 'Nolita's job' that had done the trick; she secretly congratulated herself for thinking of this angle, and was relieved Elsie didn't question it.

'All right, off you go,' she whispered, shooing Elsie on.

Rorie watched her go, fingers crossed as she hoped and prayed that no harm would come to her. Again she glanced anxiously at the surveillance camera, then decided she wasn't going to worry about it; thinking back to life at Poker Bute Hall, she remembered that just having a camera pointed at you didn't necessarily mean anyone was actually *watching*. Near the emergency exit was a spiral staircase, which appeared to provide the only access to any other parts of the building. Rorie made her way down it, adopting the same glazed expression she had used at the silk farm; a look that said, 'Here I am, same as every other day, boring old work.' The expression that was on everyone else's face as well.

At the same time, Rorie tried to take in as much as she could of what was going on around her. The machines did indeed seem to be weaving the silk into fabric. Fabric for churning out ever more new fashions, week after week. Rorie thought of all those women out there, slavishly discarding their weekly wardrobe in favour of the latest thing, which itself would only last a week. She couldn't help wondering who else Rexco would be commandeering by now, to do the job Nolita used to do. Clothing was no more permanent than the weekly grocery shopping; Rorie and Elsie had grown up with that. It was just the way things *were*...

Rorie made her way across the factory floor; nobody gave her a second glance. *D32*, said the voice in her head: whatever that was, she needed to find it. Just as she had this thought, she spotted the number D24 above one of the workstations. *No!* A factory workstation, manned by drones? That couldn't be what she was after. Could it? A few paces further, and she was at number D26...well, of course she had to check it out, but this was ridiculous. It simply wasn't possible! No way could her parents just be obediently working away at these machines, it didn't...

Then, she saw them. Two figures, just up ahead; both dark-haired – the man a little more grey than the woman. And yes, the number of the station was D32. Rorie couldn't contain herself. 'Mum! Dad!' she cried, running towards them. Everyone, including the two at station D32, turned to her.

She stopped in her tracks. The two faces stared back at her. Dad's face: the same creases around his eyes, same deep furrows running from either side of his prominent nose to the corners of his mouth, same well-defined chin. Mum's face: the same sweeping arch to her brows, same startling blue eyes, same mole on her cheek. All of the features were in the right place, but these were not Mum and Dad: they were mere husks.

Not a flicker of recognition. The horror of the moment sent a shooting pain through Rorie's bones, like lightning all over again. Followed swiftly by a hysterical bubble of laughter. 'Oh, but *of course* you don't know me!' she exclaimed. 'I mean, I'm...' She looked down at her Maggie overall, her Maggie hands. 'Different.'

All the same, this felt deeply troubling. *But my eyes*, said the voice in her head. *I'm still me inside. Can't you tell?*

A parent should be able to see. But these two... If

the eyes were the windows to the soul, then these two souls consisted of little more than plain floorboards and blank, off-white walls. No fire crackling in the grate, no sparkle of inspiration.

'Different?' said the man. 'I'm sorry, different from what?'

His hair, she noticed, was neatly combed, with a side parting. Not Dad's usual just-got-out-of-bed look.

'Why did you just call us "Mum and Dad"?' asked the woman. Perfect, neat ponytail. When Mum tied her hair back, she usually coiled it up and clamped it vaguely in place, all messy and tumbling.

What she said next turned Rorie to ice:

'We haven't got any children.'

Chapter 15
Cocoon

Elsie hurried along the platform outside the emergency exit and down the spiral staircase. Heading over the grassy verge, she made a beeline for some shrubbery, where she quickly concealed herself. The huge building – one of a cluster of four – looked like a giant shiny pebble jutting out of the hillside. Mounted high over the complex, towards the top of the ridge, great white vertical pillars supported cone-shaped devices, like the engines on an aeroplane's wings; Elsie knew these were wind turbines. In the other direction was a car park, and directly ahead of her was the sweep of the grand driveway at the front of the complex.

She sat and waited. Nobody came or went from the main entrance. All she could hear was muted factory noise merged with the hum of nearby motorway traffic, and the occasional grunt and splutter of trucks coming and going from the depot, way at the back. Fear and anxiety ebbed away, and before long Elsie realised she was bored. She picked up a stick and began digging at the earth with it, wondering what was going on inside by now. Every now and then she looked up and gazed around, but still nothing happened. What was *supposed* to happen?

This was not much of a job.

Well, thought Elsie, *there's no one around, so it won't matter if I explore a bit.* She got up and wandered. The grounds surrounding the complex were covered in fine, sandy gravel that peppered her shoes with whitish dust. Paths led between beds of banana, rubber and bird-of-paradise plants, as well as something else with an intoxicating scent. Poking out here and there from among the plants were some other sort of pillar, much smaller than the turbines. Elsie peered over at the building; she couldn't help speculating as to how she might sneak back in. But then, as she stepped forwards, she felt a weird sensation, as if an invisible elastic band were holding her back. She felt around, and her fingers closed on some sort of thread pressing into her waist. She pulled it – it was strong and stretchy, yet so light as to be barely there. It was translucent and shiny, like gossamer, or...well, like silk. Strange – where had that come from? It was stuck to a nearby plant. Elsie tugged, and it came away attached to a leaf. She wrapped it around her hand like a cat's cradle, gazing in wonder. It was beautiful stuff, catching the light in rainbow colours. The thread led across the path to the other flowerbed; Elsie followed it, gathering it around her wrist as she went.

Now here was another thread; Elsie took hold of that too, winding it around her other hand. It was an aimless pursuit, yet strangely calming. On and on she went, gathering the thread. Perhaps she didn't mind being out here after all. Rorie would contact her if she was needed. Meanwhile, she would play with the silk. Follow the thread, see where it leads...

The industrial hum of the factory had a pulsing quality to it – rhythmic, soothing. The sweet perfume of the flowers, the heat of the day...it all felt quite dreamlike now. The silk was so scintillating, entrancing. She wound it around and around, gathering...

The silk was around her middle. How had that happened? She must have been collecting another thread around her waist as she went. She retraced her steps so as to disentangle herself, but somehow another thread wound itself around her ankle. She bent over to pull at it; it stretched but it wouldn't break. She straightened up, only to find that a thread had draped itself over her head. She pulled at that, but now they seemed to be coming at her from all directions.

'Help!' she cried.

Hmm-hmm, went the industrial noise from all around.

A crow flapped and took off, cawing.

Three men stood over Rorie. Two of them were armed.

'Who are you?' asked one of them. 'What are you doing here?'

Rorie gulped hard. They had appeared before she'd had a chance to collect her thoughts. 'I…I have private business with Mr and Mrs Stemphior.'

'I didn't ask that,' retorted the man. 'I said, who *are* you?'

Rorie stared at him, eyes burning. She turned back pleadingly to Mum and Dad, but they just stood there, bemused.

'All right!' she cried, all her pain now channelled into rage. 'If you must know, my name is Rorie Silk,

and I happen to know that these are my parents—'
Her voice broke up at the end of the sentence. She
took a deep breath. 'And what *I'd* like to know is,
what have you done to their minds?'

The man viewed her dispassionately as she spoke
out, as did his companions. But one tiny, sharp intake
of breath at the mention of the name 'Silk' told Rorie
all she needed to know: this man was in on the
conspiracy.

'I'm very sorry, sir,' said the Dad-shaped person, in
an uncharacteristically meek tone, 'but we really don't
understand what she's talking about.'

Another shooting pain through Rorie's bones. This
was Dad! This *was* Dad...

'Don't worry about it,' replied the man. He turned
to Rorie. 'You're coming with me.'

Rorie could contain herself no longer. 'No! No, no,
no! These are my *parents*,' she sobbed. 'What have
you *done* to them?'

The two armed men took hold of her and together
they led her away. Rorie fought with all her might,
craning her neck round to see her parents. In
a desperate last-ditch attempt to connect, she yelled,
'You *do* have children – Rorie and Elsie. These people
stole your lives; you've got to get them back!'

Chapter 16
Tyra Spinorba

They took her bag from her straight away. 'No, I must have that!' she protested. 'My...medicines,' she added, desperately clinging on as it was pulled away. 'I need them!'

The man yanked forcefully, releasing the bag from her grip. He reached inside, took out the remains of Aunt Irmine's jacket, and grinned sarcastically. 'Pull the other one!'

Rorie felt the panic rise in her throat. 'You don't understand, it's... You've got no right!'

'Oh, but we *have*,' the man asserted. 'You, on the other hand, have no right to be here.'

Rorie could do nothing but look on helplessly as he slung the bag casually over his shoulder. She felt like a hermit crab, caught naked and vulnerable without its shell. The contents of that bag were all she had to protect her, and in a heartbeat she was without them. How on earth was she going to escape now, with identity-change no longer an option?

She was escorted down a long corridor into the building's nerve centre, eventually coming to a domed, hexagonal room. It was softly lit, the only natural daylight coming from a circular skylight in the centre of the ceiling. Sunbeams slanted through it at an angle; a large meeting table stood immediately below it. A muted green glow also came from a large aquarium that extended along one of the six walls. Two gigantic mottled red crabs with incredibly long, spidery legs dominated its inhabitants. In the shadows, Rorie could just make out a figure in a lab coat sitting at a desk, apparently monitoring some data on a screen. And in the foreground, a heavy-set woman stood beside the large table. Her black hair was wound into tight, chunky corkscrews, which stood out from her scalp like a gorgon's snake-hair. She turned and shifted into the soft beam of light, and her face was revealed.

Rorie gasped; this was not what she'd expected. 'Misty?' she said uncertainly. It was true, there was a strong resemblance: the same moon-face, same rosebud lips, same tiny, black-rimmed eyes. But there was a difference, too; she was heavier, and looked older.

'Ah, you think you know who I am, of course,' said the woman. 'But you don't. I, however, know exactly who *you* are, despite your, uh…disguise. You are Rorie Silk, and I want to thank you.'

'*Thank* me?'

The woman smiled. There was that same quiet serenity about her manner – the soft, soothing voice that had been so entrancing, so hypnotic. 'Yes. For being so helpful. You made it so easy for me to bring you here – you and your little sister.'

Elsie! 'Where is she?' cried Rorie. 'And if you're not Misty, who are you?'

'Don't worry about Elsie,' said the woman. 'She got a little tangled up, but she's on her way. Why don't you have a seat while you wait, and take your overall off?'

Rorie's eyes lowered.

The woman chuckled. 'Not comfortable changing in front of others? Don't worry! We *know*, Rorie. We all know about your powers of transformation. We know all about the incident with the lightning flash and everything – we found out from your uncle. Go on! Take it off.' She stepped forwards and held out her hand.

Part of Rorie wanted to remove the overall anyway – her alarm that these enemies knew her secret was tempered by the fact that she desperately wanted to be out of the Maggie guise; all the anxiety was making the invisible steel bands tighten around her chest again. But as she took off the overall, she attempted to retrieve the Shel and the miniature camera from its pocket.

The woman wagged her finger at her. 'Uh-uh-uh! We'll have those too.'

Rorie reluctantly handed them over.

'Thank you,' said the woman. She stared closely at Rorie, waiting for the change. Then, as subtle movements began to reshape Rorie's nose, her cheeks, her brow, the woman sighed in admiration. 'Well, well. Remarkable.'

Rorie closed her eyes, willing the changes to speed up. They took so long! At least her chest wasn't getting any worse.

'Ah, here she is!' said the woman.

Rorie opened her eyes and saw Elsie being brought in by two more men, struggling to free herself from a tangle of silk that had completely enveloped her. 'Let me outta here!' she was yelling. Rorie instinctively lurched towards her, but was held back.

'Don't worry,' said the woman. 'We'll sort her out.' She stifled a laugh. 'Oh, sorry, but it is so very *satisfying*... Cut her loose!' she commanded, then turned back to Rorie. 'While they're doing that, I'll introduce myself. My name is Tyra Spinorba. Misty is one of what I call my "avatars" – I do so hate the word "clone", don't you?'

Rorie's eyes widened. 'She's your *clone*?'

'Tut-tut-tut,' said Tyra, and Rorie was reminded of this mannerism of Misty's. 'I said *avatar*,' corrected Tyra. Then, with a flutter of her hand, she added, 'But yes, that is the scientific term. And you noticed one thing: that her name could also be read as "Miss T", the name you found on the Minimerica computer. Unfortunately, you took a look at the work Misty had done with Nolita and jumped to the conclusion that she was the "Miss T" responsible for running Minimerica. Wrong! In fact it referred to the *original* Miss T, as in "Miss Tyra", as in me. Ha ha! You had the wrong person arrested! Tut-tut. Poor Misty...and she was doing so well.'

Rorie could hardly believe what she was hearing. 'Hold on. You said Misty's *one* of your avatars? How many are there?'

'I don't have to tell you that!' retorted Tyra. She turned and gazed pensively at the aquarium, apparently communing with one of the giant crabs. It tilted backwards, revealing its freakish alien underside with its ten divisions for those incredible long, spindly legs. 'It's feeding time, Frances,' said Tyra. The lab-coated figure nodded and disappeared.

'My father was a great entrepreneur, a very powerful man,' Tyra went on. 'The founder of Rexco. The avatars were his idea. He persuaded his scientists to clone him, and the result was a boy slightly younger than me. Alas, at that time the technique had not yet been perfected, and my broth – the boy, I should say – died at the age of nine. It's very strange growing up with your father's avatar, you know; like a brother, and yet...not. After he died, the scientists determined that a clone would have a better chance of a decent lifespan if they used cells from a young person. So they used me. I am twelve years older than my avatars.'

'I couldn't care less about your stupid avatars,' Rorie spat. 'I only care about my family!' She glanced at Elsie, who was now emerging, whimpering, from her tangled cocoon of silk, then turned back to Tyra. 'What have you done to our parents?'

'Your parents are fine; they are both in excellent health.'

'What the hell are you talking about? They're our mum and dad! You took them away! And how come nobody's reported them – ah, I suppose all the other people here are zombiefied, too?'

Tyra winced. 'Really, Rorie, you must try not to be so *aggressive*. Otherwise I shall have to administer treatment.' She emerged from behind the table, and Rorie saw that she was holding a device that she recognised only too well. It was identical to the one Misty had used on the ex-celebs – a sort of tattoo gun, it implanted a microchip that helped Misty to erase memories completely from the mind of the subject.

Rorie was helpless; with so many men to restrain her and Elsie, it would be very easy for Tyra to go right ahead and implant them. Which made Rorie wonder why she hadn't done so straight away. 'Well, what are you waiting for?' she said. 'You want us unaltered for some reason – what is it?'

Tyra acted as if she hadn't heard. She appeared to be deep in thought as she watched Frances lowering dead fish into the aquarium. 'The trouble with cloning,' she said at last, 'is all that waiting around. For *years*. A whole childhood and adolescence! It just takes too long. You want more clever people, you want them *now*.'

'But you've destroyed their minds!' protested Rorie, as she tried not to look at the monster crabs devouring their lunch. 'What's the good of that?'

Elsie's face was the picture of pure desolation. 'They have?'

'Yes,' said Rorie. 'Mum and Dad are here, but in body only. They don't even know they ever had children!'

Elsie gasped in horror.

'Sorry about that,' said Tyra, as if she were apologising for accidentally treading on someone's toe. 'Well, now I've got you where I want you, thanks to your kind co-operation. 'That really was easy!'

'You *meant* us to come here?' asked Elsie.

'Yes, I was just telling your sister,' said Tyra. 'Ha ha! So touchingly naive, the way you thought you'd outwitted the Zedforce men back in that place in Wales, with that little "disguise" of yours, Rorie! Don't you think they'd have been informed of your powers of transformation? Misty told me all about it as soon as she could. I mean, of *course* she did! Don't you think we talk? You didn't really think this through, did you?'

Rorie felt her face flush; no, she supposed she hadn't. Nor had Nolita, for that matter. No wonder Zedforce had come back and closed off Kethly Merwiden.

'So, of course, O'Brien and his team were briefed,' Tyra went on smugly. 'I showed them pictures of your normal appearance, when not in disguise…and explained that when you made your transformations, you didn't change completely.' She approached the table and touched a control. A large screen on the back wall sprang to life, filled with an image of Rorie-as-'Livia'. 'This is a picture O'Brien took of you using the spy camera on his lapel.'

Rorie tried to recall seeing this device on O'Brien, but couldn't. It was obviously some variation of the camera brooch Gula had lent her – the one she didn't have any more.

'However, he couldn't be a hundred per cent sure he had the person he was after,' Tyra continued. 'So O'Brien returned the next day and did a little further investigation into the person you were disguised as. Wasn't too hard – I gather there was a young girl who was very helpful.'

Elsie groaned loudly. 'Oh, must've been Dream!'

'That's right,' confirmed Tyra. 'Well, once O'Brien knew that the room he met you in belonged to someone called Lilith, he made a point of meeting her. He was then able to take her picture without her knowing. These two images were then run through a morphing program, and this is what it came up with…'

The screen now filled with a normal image of Rorie. Then, through a series of minute changes, the facial features gradually became more like those of Lilith. When the changes stopped, the resultant image was shown alongside the previous one, that of Rorie-as-'Livia'. They were almost identical.

'As you can see,' said Tyra, 'once they'd done that, they were able to say with absolute certainty where Rorie Silk was. Then it was just a case of making it easy for you to find your way here. Which, as I say, you co-operated with perfectly.'

'Oh *right*,' remarked Rorie sarcastically. 'Like, you knew I'd infiltrate De Lusse, and find out where—'

'We knew it wouldn't take you long to figure out the De Lusse/Rexco connection,' interrupted Tyra. 'Kindergarten stuff! And the whole disguise thing; obviously you were going to do that. Oh, and did you really think we'd have been so stupid as to have changed your parents' names to "Stemphior"? Bit of an obvious clue, don't you think? That was planted for you to pick up on. The supervisor deliberately gave you lots of time to figure it all out. *Ages*.'

'OK, so if O'Brien knew who I really was, why didn't he just take me away?'

'*Because*, my dear, that would have been illegal.

You seem to have forgotten that Zedforce are a police force.'

'No, they're not, they're thugs!' retorted Elsie.

Tyra rolled her eyes and wandered nonchalantly back to the aquarium. Still Rorie tried to avert her eyes from the spectacle of the monstrous crabs as they tore the little fish to shreds. But the slow dance of those gigantic spider legs, the fluttering of crustacean mouthparts, and the snapping of pincers – which themselves resembled the sharp-beaked heads of murderous prehistoric birds – was all horribly compelling.

Tyra turned. 'Zedforce *are*, in fact, a highly specialised investigative police force. And in this instance, they were put in a very difficult position: two minors had engaged in a subversive act more egregious than many spies manage in a lifetime.'

Rorie felt an inner glow of pride at this reference to their exposing of Minimerica; Tyra had, inadvertently, paid them a huge compliment.

'But you are, as I say, minors. And due to your ability to change your appearance so radically, Rorie, even if arrest were an option, proof of your guilt in court would have been extremely difficult. Some people we would want to use as witnesses – Max and

Lonnie Bix, for example – have only seen you in a different guise. So you see, it would have been complicated.'

'Not to mention the fact that you don't want people to know why you were keeping Minimerica so secret in the first place,' said Rorie. 'I see Rexco managed to gloss over all of that.'

Again, Tyra ignored Rorie's remark. She turned and contemplated a giant crab as it devoured a particularly large fish. 'All right, men, you can lock them up now. I've got meetings to arrange.'

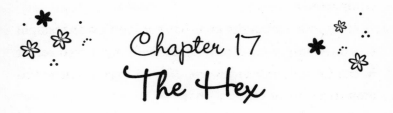

Chapter 17
The Hex

'OK, you: out,' said the man. Rorie blinked at him, confused. This person didn't look or sound like Bilbo, or any of the other Kethly Merwiden people. Then with a cold, clammy sensation she realised where she was. She propped herself up, and found that she ached all over. She had been awake almost all night, and was amazed to find that she'd slept at all.

Elsie began to cry the instant her eyes were open. Rorie put her arm around her. 'OK, Else, sshh.'

'Out!' snapped the man impatiently.

The iron-barred cell was tiny, and stuck in the corner of a stinking, neon-lit laboratory. The smell came from a mixture of things, some of which Rorie couldn't identify, and others – like monkeys – that she could. The monkeys, separated into solitary cages, either stared listlessly into the distance, or paced frantically back and forth. What were they for? Rorie wasn't sure she wanted to find out.

After a breakfast of cold, cardboard toast and bruised, over-ripe bananas – *monkey food*, thought Rorie – they were brought back to Tyra Spinorba's headquarters, the Hex. Apparently it was called this because of its hexagonal shape – though given the way Tyra had cast a virtual spell, or hex, over her parents, Rorie couldn't help thinking how horribly appropriate the name was. Could that spell be broken? That was what she needed to find out.

Tyra was by the aquarium, her face flooded with blue light as she stood talking to her weasel-faced assistant, Frances. The giant orange spider crabs danced behind them. 'Ah, hello,' said Tyra, looking up. 'Did you sleep well?'

'We're not monkeys,' Elsie retorted, 'so why are you treating us like them?'

Tyra came forward. 'I'm treating you,' she replied, her tiny black eyes smouldering, 'like the criminals that you are.'

'You stole our parents!' cried Rorie. 'What could be more criminal than that?'

'No, that is where you are wrong,' corrected Tyra. 'Like you, they came to us of their own accord.'

'*What have you done to them?*' Rorie demanded once again.

'Let me ask *you* something,' suggested Tyra. 'Suppose you're voyaging in the frozen wastes of Antarctica. You suffer frostbite, and discover you have gangrene. You must either remove a couple of rotten toes, or risk losing your whole leg and possibly dying. Which is better?'

Rorie scowled at her. 'I hope you're not likening our parents to a pair of rotten toes!'

'Hmm, not the best analogy, I admit; perhaps cancerous cells would be closer. Cells that think they can invent a new way for cells to behave...'

'That's despicable! Our parents were always good, law-abiding people—'

'And what do you think would happen to society if nobody ever needed new clothes, hmm?' asked Tyra, those jet eyes now aflame. 'Oh, all that rot about "saving the planet" by drastically cutting down on production! What happens to the people who grow and mill the cotton, who manufacture other materials, whose whole *livelihoods* depend on the industry? Millions of lives, *missy* – millions!'

'That's no reason to destroy lives!'

'No? Not to cut out a cancer before it spreads?'

'You don't care about the people!' yelled Elsie. 'What about Minimerica?'

'Yeah, what about the lives of all those people?' Rorie added. 'What about Poker Bute Hall? How many other schools for drones do you run? Are you trying to turn the whole population into zombies?'

At Tyra's nod, two men came forward and took hold of the girls' arms.

'What you regard as "zombies",' said Tyra, 'others might call "useful members of society". And happy ones, too – I don't suppose you found a great deal of suffering on Minimerica, did you?'

'*Happy?*' sneered Rorie. 'About as happy as…as somebody stuck in a virtual reality game for ever and ever! We know you were putting stuff in the food, in the air, into their minds: controlling them. Same with Poker Bute Hall! One person steps out of line, shows a bit of individuality, and *boom!* They're carted off to an "anger management course", and when they come back it's like they're…I don't know, it's like they've had part of their brain removed!'

'Those anger management courses have been highly praised by several head teachers,' replied Tyra. 'The trouble with you is that you think there's something admirable about being different just for the sake of it.

You've been conditioned to think that way by your domineering parents. It isn't the view most people hold, you know.'

Rorie groaned in disgust. She thought wistfully of Mum's story about the tiger-lilies. How like the king in that story Tyra Spinorba was! Bit by bit, she was bleaching out all individuality from more and more people, forcing them to conform to her idea of how they should be, the way that suited Big Business.

And it was at that moment that Rorie realised something: that no matter how impossible it might seem now, she was in a unique position to do something about it, because she knew so much more than anyone else about what Tyra was up to. Tyra had as good as confessed to being a megalomaniac! And it was down to Rorie to play the role of tiger-lily to all those poor bleached-out souls. The only question was, how?

'You're right, however,' said Tyra. 'I *could* just implant you right now, and rid Rexco of the single most irritating flea in its fur.' She came forward, her tiny eyes glittering with malice. 'So, why don't I?' She paused for effect as she walked round Rorie, eyeing her up and down. Her locks of hair bounced gently as she walked – not so much like gorgon snakes, thought Rorie now;

more like the furry black legs of a tarantula. 'Haven't figured it out yet, hmm?' There was that small, enigmatic china-doll smile. Frances, who had been very much in the background until now, moved forwards, carrying a clipboard, a small tray of test tubes and some other items Rorie couldn't make out.

'Missss Chameleon Girl,' whispered Tyra. 'How do you do it? That's what I want to know.'

'I don't *know* how I do it!' said Rorie.

Tyra exchanged a look with Frances, who had now put the things down on the table and was pulling on some latex gloves. Frances' pale eyes were too close together, and her forehead was strangely prominent. Her mouth was little more than a thin gash under a sharp nose, and she had a large mole on her left cheek.

'Perhaps not,' said Tyra. 'But I'm sure there are ways we can investigate...run some tests.'

Frances reached for Rorie's arm.

'You're not running any tests on my sister!' yelled Elsie. 'What's it got to do with you, anyway?'

'Did I say *single* most irritating flea?' said Tyra, turning to Elsie. 'I should have said two. And actually, there's nothing to stop me implanting *you* right now, missy.'

'No!' cried Rorie. 'You leave her alone...Elsie, I can

deal with this, OK?' She turned back to Tyra. 'But Elsie has a point. What *has* it got to do with you?'

'I don't have to answer that. So, if you're not going to explain how you change, we'll have to run some blood tests. You won't come to any harm; we just need samples, before and after.'

Suddenly, Rorie caught a glimpse of a way in which she might stand a chance of escaping after all. 'Before and after? You mean, before and after I change? Right, well then, you'll have to let me put on something from my bag, won't you?' Yes! Perhaps it should be the linings from the Nikki Deeds trainers; they would do nicely if she wanted to fight her way out of here. There would be a few people to fend off, but...well, it was a start. She was sure Tyra still didn't know about the way she was able to take on other people's abilities.

'Oh, I'm *so* sorry,' said Tyra. 'We destroyed those.'

Rorie's heart did a flip. Destroyed! All of those things...even the Elvis pendant! No matter how much she hated changing, it still felt as if she'd had a limb removed.

'But we don't need them,' added Tyra. 'We have that overall you were wearing before—'

'No, not that!' protested Rorie. 'I...that is...' She stalled as she wondered what she could afford to give away about the asthma. It wasn't explaining the nature of the change she was worried about – as she'd realised when she'd had to tell Nolita, it was only a *physical* change, not a skill. No: what she didn't like was having to admit that putting certain things on made her ill. That would give her enemy ammunition.

'And why not?' prompted Tyra.

'It...the effect wears out. It only works once with each thing,' replied Rorie, then instantly regretted it.

Tyra raised an eyebrow. 'Oh? So why did you suggest a moment ago that you use something from your backpack? Presumably those are things you've used before?'

Rorie thought. Even if she denied it, tests would prove otherwise. She had no choice but to come clean. 'OK. The overall makes me ill. It gives me asthma, because its owner has asthma.' There. Now they could do what they wanted to her.

'Ah, *interesting*,' said Tyra. Frances jotted down some notes. 'Well, let's try something from a healthy person,' Tyra added. 'Since we want you well. For now.'

Rorie didn't like the use of the words 'for now' one little bit.

Chapter 18
The Mole

'Rorie, wake up, pleeease!'

'Wha—?' Rorie gazed at her sister, bleary-eyed. 'Oh, leave me alone.' She turned over and pulled the thin blanket over her head.

'No, I'm not gonna leave you alone. They sent me in here 'cause they want me to bring you round.'

'Don't care,' came Rorie's muffled response.

'You've been asleep fourteen hours! Something's gone wrong, but we don't know what. Oh, Rorie, when you gonna change back? Please be you...*please*. You're all I've got, and we still gotta get Mum'n'Dad!'

The words floated around in Rorie's head, disconnected from one another. *Change back?* she thought abstractly. *Have I not changed back?* It wasn't alarm she felt, but merely the sort of mild bewilderment and annoyance of not being able to get the toaster to work. And there was something else bothering her, too...oh yes, Mum and Dad. Must do something about that. *Later. Oh, so tired...*

Rorie awoke in darkness. With an awful heaviness, she remembered where she was. She had no idea what time it was, but everything was still and silent; it had to be the middle of the night. Then, carrying an even more awful weight, came the full recollection of the Big Change: Tyra Spinorba handing her a cardigan belonging to Frances; Rorie herself being forced to put it on. Then the nausea: much worse this time – Rorie had been sick. Then the sensation of shrinking, of becoming ugly like the beady-eyed Frances...

The nausea had subsided. Yet Rorie had felt...not all there. Like a ghost.

Blood samples had been taken before and after; also snippets of hair. She was put through a whole-body scanner twice. She was filmed and photographed. Her iris was analysed. They made sound recordings of her normal voice and her changed voice. They took all sorts of measurements. Frances bombarded her with questions about the transformations. What were the physical sensations? Had she ever experienced any other kinds of illness or infirmity through transformations?

Was her motivation affected? Frances tested her on her own interests, likes and dislikes. Nothing too revealing – just favourite foods, music and so on. Finally, the cardigan had come off.

And...nothing had happened.

Rorie was stuck in Frances-mode.

They waited and waited; nothing. Gripped by panic, Rorie had demanded a mirror. The real Frances produced a small round one. Rorie stared till she almost went cross-eyed. There, still, were those close-together eyes, the thin lips, the mole. She had stared and stared at that mole; *surely* it would soon fade? But no: everything remained stubbornly the same.

'What have you done to me?' she'd cried. 'This isn't supposed to happen...I'm supposed to change back! It's that scanner, isn't it? The radiation... Oh, what have you *done*?'

It was too dark now for Rorie to see – and besides, there was no mirror in the cell. Trembling, she ran her fingers over her head and face...yes! Her hair felt thicker, more like her own; her nose seemed back to normal, but then...feeling her left cheek, she found a small bump. The mole. It was still there.

'Elsie! Psst, Elsie!' Rorie shook her sister urgently.

Elsie woke in no time. 'Rorie! You're awake!'

'Yes, but am I me?'

'I dunno, I can't see...' She peered closer. 'Yes! I fink you are! Except...' She reached up, touched the mole. 'What's that? Is it...?'

Rorie sighed. 'Frances' mole. Yes, I know. It won't go away.'

'Oh, but you're *you* again!' cried Elsie, throwing her arms around her middle. She began to sob. 'I was so scared! I thought my Rorie was gone...gone!'

Rorie was just as overcome. 'Oh, me too! It was horrible! Thank God...just think, I might have been stuck "being" Frances for *ever*...my life wouldn't have been worth living!' The elation she felt was like pure nectar coursing through her veins. How she could feel so ridiculously happy at a time like this, she couldn't fathom – but she was. Well, almost. 'But will this mole ever go away?'

'I don't care, I don't care!' wailed Elsie. 'You're you!'

'Sshh!' hissed Rorie. 'We don't want anyone coming in, seeing what all the commotion's about.'

'OK, sorry,' whispered Elsie.

Rorie took a deep breath. They sat in silence for a moment.

'You know something,' said Rorie, after a while. 'This mole...it makes me wonder.'

Elsie sniffed loudly. 'What?'

'Well, if that's a permanent change, then maybe there are other kinds of permanent change, too – ones I don't know about yet. Internal ones.'

'What, you mean, like your intestines and stuff?'

'No – well, yes, that too, but...what I'm talking about is skills – things Frances can do, but I can't.'

'Oh, right! Like with the Nikki Deeds trainers and stuff. So how d'you find out?'

'I haven't a clue...but I'm also wondering if there's anything left behind from the last couple of transformations as well...'

'Like what?' Elsie said.

'I'm not sure,' said Rorie. 'But...oh boy, I've just had a thought.'

'What?'

'OK, there's this thing I learnt from Lilith...' Rorie explained all about auras, what they were and what she understood about the different colours, and how she had seen them herself.

Elsie listened, engrossed. Then she frowned. 'OK, but even if you *could* make yourself see auras again, what use would it be?'

'That's just it!' said Rorie. 'I think I know! You see, auras don't stay the same all the time; the colours in them change, they become brighter or duller...apparently, if you get really good at tuning into them, you can actually read people's thoughts. And now I think about it, I've seen someone's thoughts played out in their aura already.'

'You have? When?'

'Remember I told you that Nolita lied to O'Brien – she said she wanted to help Zedforce and Rexco by working undercover? Well, I had a lot of thoughts jamming up my head at the time – I'd only just got away with disguising myself in front of the Zedforce guys, so my mind wasn't really focused on it. But now, looking back, I've realised something: Nolita's aura gave away the lie before she'd even said anything.'

Elsie's eyes gleamed in the darkness. 'It did?'

'Yes, because a split second before, I saw a pattern of dark-pink shooting shapes radiating from her head. Don't you see? That was the lie forming itself.'

'So now you can tell if someone's lying?'

'Yes...I mean no...I mean, I don't know. The point is that I *might* be able to – with practice. Lilith said anyone can learn, and she told me a lot about technique. Plus, if I have any Lilith-ness still in me...well, maybe that could help, too.'

Elsie's brow creased even more. 'I still don't see what use it would be...'

'Listen, it's not much, I know,' admitted Rorie. 'Hey, I'm not sure how it can help us either – or even if it can help at all. But it's worth thinking about. I mean, what else do we have?'

Elsie gazed around the tiny cell and sighed. 'Nothing, I guess.'

'And I'll tell you what else,' said Rorie. 'We need to find out as much as we can about exactly what's going on here. Like, did you notice the Hex has five doors leading from it? We know where two of them go, but where do you suppose the other three lead? And I've been wondering, what do they want with you?'

Elsie shrugged. 'They din't want me lurking about.'

'Yes, I know, but why haven't they implanted you yet? Something's stopping them, and I want to know what it is. Oh, and why do you suppose Tyra's so keen to find out how I change? She must want to be able to reproduce that process for her own uses – but what do you suppose those are?'

'Well, that's ovvious!' said Elsie.

Rorie blinked at her. 'It is?'

'Yeah! She's jealous. She wants to be able to change, too. Who wouldn't?'

'Oh, *Elsie*. Really, it's not as if she's some seven-year-old kid who...hang on. Maybe you've got something there.'

'Course I have.'

'No, I mean...well, there was all that stuff about her "avatars" – she wouldn't say how many there were. I guess she must have them scattered in different parts of the world, all doing the same kind of job as Misty: controlling key figures like Nolita. And all of them identical. Well, think about it; that could be a bit of a drawback, couldn't it?'

'Oh yeah. I guess you'd want to change them a bit.'

'Which you can do, of course, with cosmetic surgery, but that's a big thing to go through, and takes weeks to recover from. How much quicker and easier this would be! And what's more, you could change any number of times. I mean, it's like Tyra was saying about me – how they couldn't arrest me, because different people saw me in different identities. If an avatar could change like that, they could easily stay ahead of anyone who got suspicious about what they were up to.'

Elsie was quiet for a moment. 'I still don't

understand what Tyra's doing with the monkeys.'

Rorie frowned. 'Hmm. Me neither...I mean, how long have they known about my transformations? I can see why they'd want to experiment on monkeys if they were researching *that*, but...something tells me they've had them here for longer than that, and there's a bigger picture here. Oh, it's so frustrating! This whole Rexco business is like...like a huge puzzle, only with pieces missing. We've got no choice but to guess at what shape those pieces are. There's some other reason for those monkeys...and I'll bet you anything that whatever it is, it's connected to what they're up to with Mum and Dad.'

'How we gonna figure it out, then?' asked Elsie.

Rorie heaved a sigh. 'I haven't a clue.'

Chapter 19
Shapeshifting

The next day came six words from Tyra that Rorie really did not want to hear:

'We need to run further tests.'

'No!' Rorie protested. 'No way am I changing back again; you must be crazy! Look what happened to me! That's never happened before.'

'Do you seriously think I care about that?' sneered Tyra. 'I don't care if you change into an ape! Hmm...come to think of it, can you do animal changes?'

Rorie didn't answer. Instead, she stared hard at Tyra, focusing all her energies on trying to see her aura. There was a sort of layer surrounding her, but Rorie couldn't tell if it was just an optical illusion or not.

'Well, there's one way to find out,' said Tyra.

Suddenly, Rorie snapped back to the conversation, and realised what Tyra was talking about. 'Forget it.

I've tried already,' she lied. 'It doesn't work.'

A ripple effect framing Tyra at that moment...or had Rorie imagined it? One way or another, she could sense irritation, suspicion and frustration.

'Well, it's beside the point, anyway,' said Tyra. She approached Rorie with Frances' cardigan. 'So let's just stick with this, shall we?'

Rorie ducked out of the way. Tyra's men came forward. 'You have to wait!' Rorie insisted, pushing Tyra's hand away. 'Give me twenty-four hours.'

Tyra shook her head and advanced again. 'You're just stalling. Hoping someone'll come and rescue you? Forget it!'

Redness. Rorie was sure she saw dark, muddy red surrounding Tyra at that moment. Anger.

'Who else besides a few people on a Welsh mountainside have any idea where you are?' challenged Tyra. 'Nobody. And there's no way your friends will get past Zedforce anyway.'

'All the same,' said Frances, touching Tyra's arm. 'The girl's transformation back into herself has yet to complete itself. Look at the mole on her cheek. I think we'll get cleaner results if we wait a while.'

Thank you! thought Rorie. She turned her attention to Frances now – and found she was able to see her aura quite plainly. Whether it was because Rorie felt she knew her intimately, having 'been' her, or whether it was purely through her powers of concentration, she didn't know – but there it was, unmistakably: a spectrum of colours, but dominant among them was the dark green of someone who was sensitive in all the worst ways – bitter, resentful...and the lemon-yellow of a fearful, subservient character.

'Cleaner results?' echoed Tyra. She sighed. 'Oh, for heaven's sake! All right. But we don't have twenty-four hours to spare. Make it four.' She turned to the men. 'Bring her back at two pm.'

They were guarded nearly the whole morning. Then the man went out briefly; the girls seized the chance to talk.

'Hey, guess what: it works!' breathed Rorie excitedly. 'I can see her aura!'

'Oh, brilliant!' cried Elsie.

'Sshh!' Rorie covered up her mouth. 'Quiet!'

'Sorry,' whispered Elsie. 'Did you find anything out yet?'

'Well, not exactly. But it's a start.'

'Oh, and guess what else,' hissed Elsie. 'I know where one of those doors goes!'

'You do?'

'Yes. *The loo*.'

'Oh, wow. Congratulations. Yes, I'd noticed that too. Anything else earth-shattering?'

'Um...no. Except I think it's also a way out, 'cause I've seen people coming in from there who look like they just arrived.'

'OK, good point,' conceded Rorie. 'Just a shame it doesn't help us. If we ever find a way of getting out of here, the first thing we'll need to do is find Mum and Dad. So escaping through the Hex is not an option. Oh, and that also means we'll have to get away during the day while they're still here at work.'

'So not on a weekend either,' added Elsie.

'Oh boy, I can't even think about that. Hell, I don't even know what day it is! OK, so that's three down, two to go. No, hang on, I've just remembered something! They put me through this scanner thing, like a big long doughnut – horrible, it was. I'd completely forgotten about it till now, but it was in one of the rooms off the Hex – right next door to here. It was a small room, nothing else in there. So that just leaves the one to the left of the aquarium, by my reckoning. *Door number five*, Else, that's what we need to—'

'Sshh!' It was Elsie's turn to hush her sister up. 'Somebody's coming.'

Frances appeared with a tray carrying two bowls of soup. She placed it in the little compartment of the cell door designed for the purpose. 'Lunch,' she said brusquely.

'Gee, thanks,' said Rorie, equally sullen as she slid open the little door to the compartment and took the tray.

Frances peered at Rorie with her piercing, too-close-together eyes. 'Hmph. Not there yet, are we?'

Somehow this made Rorie feel as if she were a naughty schoolgirl who'd failed a test.

She watched as Frances took a clipboard down from its hook on the wall, and began surveying the monkeys and making notes.

'What are the monkeys for?' asked Elsie through the bars.

'That's *none* of your business,' muttered Frances in clipped tones, not taking her eyes off the sheet as she wrote.

Elsie, being Elsie, was undeterred. 'Do you do 'speriments on them? 'Cause you shouldn't do that, you know, it's cruel. What kinda 'speriments do you do on them?'

Frances just ignored her. She stood and stared at one of the monkeys, head to one side. Then she removed a small card from the pocket of her white coat, and swiped it down a ridge at the side of the cage. The cage door opened. Frances slipped the card back into her pocket, and took the monkey out.

Rorie and Elsie looked at each other, and Rorie could tell Elsie was thinking the same as she was. There were twelve monkeys altogether; as long as they weren't too drugged-up, twelve monkeys could create quite a bit of chaos. And she didn't think they *were* drugged-up; just driven half-mad with depression at being so confined, most likely. Just think how they might behave if they were set free after being cooped up for so long! If she could just get hold of that card...

Then Rorie had an idea. 'Get her to come over here and look at me again,' she whispered to Elsie. 'Really close.'

Elsie gave her the thumbs-up. Rorie picked up her bowl of tomato soup, slurped up a huge mouthful of it, and waited.

'Oh, miss, come quick!' cried Elsie. 'Something's happened to Rorie's face!'

Rorie sat with her back to Frances, soup-filled cheeks ballooning out like a trumpeter's, as she heard first the closing of the monkey's cage door, then the approaching steps of the curious researcher.

'What's the matter?' demanded Frances tersely. Rorie could tell she was really close now. She turned and spurted the mouthful of red soup all down the front of Frances' pristine white lab coat.

'Aargh!' Frances lurched back, dropping her clipboard. 'You disgusting child!' She reached for the small sink just inside the door, pulled off the coat and tried to rinse out the soup. 'I don't know what you're playing at,' she scolded, 'but you're not making things any easier for yourselves, I can tell you!'

Wiping her chin, Rorie watched intently as Frances finished scrubbing the coat and wrung it out, scolding her all the while. She attempted to dry it with the hand-dryer, then gave up and hung it on a hook on the back of the door.

Rorie and Elsie exchanged glances again – excitedly this time, as all it would take to retrieve that swipe card was a surreptitious dip into the coat pocket on their way back to Tyra's office...

But a split second later, they were disappointed: Frances, remembering the card, turned back and removed it from the coat pocket. Then she left the room.

They were stumped.

'Oh well, we tried,' sighed Rorie.

'Yeah,' said Elsie.

The two of them sat in grim silence. The monkeys chattered.

'Blimey, she didn't half make a big fuss over a bit of soup on her overall,' Elsie remarked disdainfully.

'Yeah,' agreed Rorie. 'The way she was scrubbing and scrubbing, like it was her best dress, or something.'

'She wouldn't need to, if she was wearing Mum'n'Dad's invention,' said Elsie. 'Come to think of it, why isn't she?'

Rorie looked at her, and her jaw fell open. 'The invention! The never-wash, shape-changing clothes…oh, Elsie, you're brilliant! Why did I never think of this before?'

'What?'

Rorie stood up and began pacing about. 'That's it, don't you see? The thing that connects everything up – the monkeys, Mum and Dad's disappearance, Tyra's interest in my chameleon changes…this is the link, the missing piece of the puzzle!'

'How's that?'

Rorie sat back down next to Elsie, and grabbed her

arm. 'OK, remember what Dad said about how the invention worked – the DNA part? Maybe you didn't take all that in, but I remember it like it was yesterday. Think about it: Dad discovered how to communicate instructions to once-live cells – like those in a sheep's wool. Well, it's probably not such a big leap from using the technology on *once*-live cells, to using it on live, human ones.'

'You mean, using the invention to change the way people look?' asked Elsie. 'But how?'

'Well, they'd have to develop the idea further, wouldn't they? Experiment. And *that* might involve using—'

'Monkeys!'

Rorie clicked her fingers. 'Exactly. Look, all this might sound extreme, but there's a logic to it. The only motive for Mum and Dad's capture that we know for sure is that Tyra doesn't want their invention to kill off the clothing industry as we know it. But there *has* to be more to all this than just that – otherwise why go to all the trouble of erasing their memories? This *fits*: Tyra's using their invention as part of her master plan to be this invisible power that runs everything, basically. Once she knew about my own ability to change – well, I must have looked to her like the goose that laid golden eggs! Already I'm someone who can change their appearance without surgery. And again, we know that this is something of great interest to Tyra Spinorba.'

'That's true.'

'Yes,' said Rorie, as she gazed at the monkeys. 'This is all about shapeshifting.'

Chapter 20
Aura of Hatred

If there was ever such a thing as black light, Rorie was looking at it right now.

Tyra's aura. Clearer now – Rorie had been practising on Elsie ever since that morning, and now it was paying off. Perhaps a little bit of Lilith was still lingering in her as well. Tyra's was unlike any other aura she had seen. There was still the redness Rorie had picked up on before, closest to Tyra's frame. But that was only one layer; much larger, extending further outwards, was the blackness, hovering there like a vacuum ready to suck up everything surrounding it.

Tyra's hand, blackness and all, came forward, holding the cardigan. Rorie had the awful sensation of being sucked into a black hole...

'One moment,' said Frances, examining Rorie closely. 'The mole – it's still there.'

Red flashes: anger. 'I don't care!' snapped Tyra. 'It's only a mole! We need to proceed.'

Black hole coming forward...

Another interruption. 'What's that chameleon doing there?' asked Elsie.

Rorie had been concentrating so hard on Tyra's aura, she hadn't noticed the caged chameleon on the table.

'It's for an experiment,' answered Tyra impatiently. She edged forwards.

Images of a rain-soaked hill filled Rorie's mind. The chameleon in her arms. The bolt of white fire from the sky...

Beside the table was a chair with strong black buckled straps attached to it. There were wires... *No!* Rorie's breath became quick, shallow. Her throat dried out. 'What sort—' She gulped hard, backing away from Tyra. 'What sort of experiment?'

'We may find that these tests on you are inconclusive,' said Tyra. 'In which case, we'll need to try out something on your sister. Along the lines of...what we know happened to you.' A tiny, gloating smile played about her lips.

Rorie exchanged a glance with Elsie. 'No. You can't—'

'Oh, I can,' insisted Tyra lightly. Her aura hovered there, black and red like glowing coals. No deception apparent; this was real.

So *that* was why they hadn't implanted Elsie yet – if all else failed, hook her up to a Frankenstein machine, zap her, and see if any changes took place.

'Rorie, I don't understand!' came Elsie's voice.

'Don't worry about it,' Rorie replied, desperately trying to sound calm and convincing. 'You won't come to any harm, Else.' She turned back to Tyra, the hatred now pulsing energetically through her veins. 'All right, answer me this: did you implant our parents with those chip things?'

A grey veil dulling the black: a holding back of information. 'I fail to see what that has to do with anything,' said Tyra.

'Oh, for heaven's sake!' snapped Rorie. 'What's it going to cost you, a little piece of information like that?'

'Put the cardigan on,' insisted Tyra. *Flashes of red anger.*

'They're our *parents*, Tyra,' said Rorie. 'Did you implant them?'

'Will you shut up!' snapped Tyra. *More flames.*

'No, I won't!' retorted Rorie. 'I've got something

you want, and I'll co-operate with you—'

'You're damned right you will!'

'But all I'm doing is asking for your co-operation in return, by answering a few harmless questions.'

'Well, I *didn't* implant them, all right?' The flames were now dampened by dark blue: concealment. But no flashes of pink, like she had seen before with Nolita. Could that mean Tyra was telling the truth? Tyra pressed forward the cardigan. 'Now put it on!'

Rorie peered at Tyra. 'And nobody else did?'

'No!' Red again – but no pink. The colours were similar – infuriatingly so – but it did look as if Tyra was telling the truth.

'OK, so how did you—'

'I'm not going to tell you!' snapped Tyra. 'Now put on the cardigan, before I have to force you—'

'The changes,' Rorie blurted out, desperate now. 'In Mum and Dad. Are they permanent...I mean, are they irreversible?'

There was a moment's pause, then Tyra's eyes glittered with malice. 'Of course they are,' she replied gloatingly.

Oh, big lie! Dark-pink shapes shooting around all over the place. Yes, yes! Oh, this was good news.

'Completely irreversible,' Tyra added. She laughed.

'I don't know what you thought you'd do about it if it weren't, but...there's nothing you can do anyway. Nothing *anyone* can do.' *Pink shapes going wild.* 'Your "Mr and Mrs Stemphior" – James and Julia Jones to the rest of us – will remain the way they are for the rest of their days. Which, of course, is as it should be.' This last remark was the only one that was not a lie; the pink shapes disappeared instantly, because although it wasn't true, Tyra believed it absolutely.

'So...once you're done with these tests on me...'

'You'll be dealt with in the same way, of course.' *Not a lie.* Tyra held out the cardigan. 'Now, *if* you please.'

Rorie glanced over at the chameleon, the wired-up chair; this was the lesser of two evils. She took the cardigan that was being foisted on her. *I'm doing this for you, Elsie. And for Mum and Dad...* But would she ever become properly herself again? Would she be stuck for ever in a half-Rorie-half-Frances existence, like she used to worry would happen if the wind changed while she was pulling a funny face? The thought was too horrible to contemplate.

Feeling like a lamb being led to the slaughter, Rorie put on the cardigan. She had just begun her descent into nausea when, doubled over and clutching her stomach, she felt something rigid in the cardigan pocket. The swipe card! Divested of her lab coat, Frances had naturally put the device for opening the monkey cages here instead. And, apparently, quite forgotten about it. So, when Elsie rushed to her sister's side to comfort her and hold her hair out of her face in case she threw up again, Rorie reached for her hand, the card concealed in the palm of her own.

Elsie slipped the card up her sleeve without anyone noticing; everyone's eyes were on Rorie. Elsie backed away, but with five people in the room besides herself and Rorie, there was only so far she was able to go before Tyra's men homed in on her. Rorie, still bent over but, thankfully, with the meagre contents of her stomach intact, was aware of this – next, she would have to create a big scene as a distraction. Well, for all Tyra and Frances knew, the transformations might sometimes produce fits, convulsions...so Rorie began to make bizarre physical jerks, as if she had no control over her body.

Tyra was clearly taken aback. 'What's the matter? What's going on?'

'She's acting up, that's what,' said Frances. 'Don't be fooled.'

This only made Rorie more determined to put on an extreme performance. She had once seen a netfilm that showed some people in a church supposedly possessed by the holy spirit. They had been quivering wildly, and uttering strange, unintelligible words. Inspired by that, she began behaving in exactly the same way, rolling her eyeballs up so only the whites showed, quivering and thrashing, muttering weird, made-up words. She found it strangely enjoyable, almost managing to forget her nausea completely.

'Rorie! Stop this!' commanded Tyra.

'Aa-uuu-tee-tee-tee!' cried Rorie, eyelids fluttering, face wild. She felt a hand grip her arm, so she flailed around even more.

'I'm not chancing anything, Frances,' Rorie could just about hear Tyra saying. 'I'm calling in Dr Visp. He needs to observe this.'

'Wee-ee-osh!' squealed Rorie, now spinning herself around like a whirling dervish. 'Mape-mape-acka-hoo!' She could only hope that Elsie understood why she was doing this, and would act on it. Though even if she did, Rorie was keenly aware that it was unlikely that her performance alone was enough to hold the attention of all five adults; something more was needed. Spotting some test tubes on the table, Rorie took advantage of the fact that Tyra was busy calling the doctor and whooshed past the table before anyone could stop her, sending the test tubes crashing to the ground. Now two of the men rushed to restrain her, while the other one joined Frances in clearing up the mess. With Tyra still on her Shel, Rorie hoped Elsie had seized the moment...meanwhile, she became positively demonic, overacting even more to compensate for the restraint.

Seconds later, Rorie knew Elsie had indeed seized the moment.

The moment contained a number of simultaneous things. It contained Tyra, panic-stricken, looking about her, saying, 'The child! Where's Elsie?'

It contained Dr Visp appearing, demanding to know what was happening with Rorie.

And it contained Rorie's realisation that Dr Visp had just left Door Number Five open behind him.

In another moment, Rorie noticed one of the men leaving to look for Elsie – and heading the wrong way! Naturally, he had assumed that the last place Elsie would make for was the cell, so instead he had gone in the direction of the factory, probably thinking that since Elsie had come from there, she would know that it led to an exit. Great!

Gradually, Rorie eased her performance. The spasms became fewer and further between – but she kept them up, so as to give the two men restraining her something to do.

'...no precedent for this,' Dr Visp, a thin, grey-looking man, was saying, 'but probably the best thing would be to sedate her.'

This alarmed Rorie; now she would really have to calm down, or risk getting a sedative injection. But she mustn't do it suddenly, or they'd be onto her. She began to droop, to soften her voice.

'Wait,' said Tyra. 'We have tests to do, and sedation will interfere with those.'

Droop, droop...

Then – hurrah! – another mad, shrieking sound came: monkeys on the loose. Elsie had done it!

'What's that noise?' asked Tyra.

'Monkeys.' Frances' face bore the look of someone who didn't quite know the meaning of the word.

'Monkeys?'

Frances turned her head in the direction of the noise. 'Um...'

Rorie could almost see the sequence of events playing itself out in Frances' mind, as she looked at the cardigan, then back at the doorway.

'OOH-OOH-AAAAHHH!' came the simian screeches, far wilder than any part of Rorie's performance.

Chapter 21
Vacant Faces

These were no drugged-up monkeys.

They were *everywhere*, going completely berserk. There seemed to be far more than twelve of them, as they bounced off the walls, screeching and whooping. Rorie saw one of the men lunge for a monkey, and in a split second the monkey, eyes flashing wildly, had sunk its teeth deep into the man's arm. Eleven others were careering this way and that, ready to do just the same. At least one of them had already weed on the floor, and this caused another of the men to slide comically and fall backwards, arms flailing.

Tyra's face was whiter than ever. She gazed around with a look of sheer disbelief, and reached down under the table for something. The next moment the air was filled with a loud siren. Frances cowered behind Tyra. Dr Visp wielded his hypodermic needle, apparently now intent on using it on a monkey – but the expression of sheer alarm on his face told quite a different story. Only one of Tyra's men remained uninjured at this point, and he certainly had his work cut out for him.

Then Elsie reappeared, awkwardly clutching some sort of bundle to her chest, but Rorie couldn't make out what it was. One of the men lunged for Elsie, but a monkey hurtled into his path, colliding with him and knocking him over. As Elsie dodged her way across the room towards her, Rorie could see that the bundle consisted of more test tubes. No sooner had she realised this, than Elsie dumped them on the floor as well – only the contents of these didn't just pool together harmlessly as the last lot had; they fizzled, and within seconds a noxious cloud had formed, making everyone cough, and making the monkeys go even more berserk than before.

There wasn't time to worry about what effect the fumes were going to have. They stank of skunks and bad eggs, but right now there was one thing they had to take advantage of, before it was too late: the cloud they had created. Stumbling through it, coughing, Rorie reached out to the small, hazy figure that was coming towards her. 'Else!' she croaked, grabbing her by the sleeve. With the siren still wailing and the monkeys shrieking like lunatics, she could speak to Elsie without being heard by anyone else. 'Go! Door number five – it's open,' she instructed between coughs. 'Get in there, and lock the door.'

'But—'

'I'll be back – I promise!' Rorie pushed Elsie towards the door, which was still ajar; Elsie disappeared behind it. Rorie could only hope she would figure out how to lock it.

Meanwhile she needed to make herself scarce. She turned on her heel, only to be confronted by two of the men. Immediately she turned back again, and headed into the epicentre of the chemical fug, but she felt a strong hand grip her arm and yank her backwards.

Rorie launched into a reprise of her crazy act, twisting and turning with all her might. The man resorted to dragging her along the floor, and no amount of thrashing about on Rorie's part was able to throw him off altogether. She craned her neck around in an attempt to bite his hand, but couldn't reach. 'Aargh!' she screamed, as an equally freaked-out monkey landed on her head, then launched off again. 'Eeeeargh!' screeched the monkey. Then Rorie noticed it was holding something: the chipgun! It seemed to want to play with it, but was bothered by the fumes. The monkey slapped its face, teeth bared in a skeletal grimace, and shook its head vigorously, as if trying to shake out the toxic mist. Finally it threw down the chipgun, which slid across the floor... Rorie stretched out her one free hand as far as she could...and got hold of it. She'd never used one before, but it seemed fairly obvious what to do. Twisting around and reaching up, she jammed the gun into the man's wrist and pulled the trigger.

The man let out a guttural howl – apparently more from shock than anything – and let go of her.

Finding that she was near the exit that led to the factory, Rorie simply threw herself out into the corridor, and she was away.

But within seconds of getting there, she could hear the pounding of feet coming towards her from the direction of the factory; probably a team responding to the alarm Tyra had set off. Rorie searched wildly for a hiding place, but the sleek, minimal space offered none. And judging by the sound of it, the response team would be appearing around the bend any moment now...

Rorie was almost paralysed with panic. Still she gazed around frantically; still she could think of nothing but turning back – yet that would never do. The walls were just smooth panels...but suddenly, a thought occurred to her; a thought that came from 'Frances', thanks to the cardigan she was still wearing – because Frances, it turned out, knew her way around here very well, and knew that if she pressed *this* panel...yes! It swung open, revealing a secret passage. Rorie threw herself into it, and the panel closed by itself.

She listened as the footsteps hurtled past. Then, when she was pretty sure there was no one still to come, she let herself out and fled down the passageway, towards the factory.

Now there was very little time: if Tyra hadn't already realised her prisoner was missing, she would do so any moment now. And she would know exactly how to trap her too: just send someone to where Mr and Mrs Stemphior – no, *Jones* – were. She knew perfectly well that Rorie wouldn't leave without them.

As she returned to workstation number D32, Rorie tried to compose herself; not easy, given her recent tousle, and the fact that she probably now reeked of skunks and bad eggs. Not to mention the fact that here were Mum and Dad, but she couldn't address them as such.

On the factory floor it was as if nothing had happened; the mayhem back in the Hex seemed like a bizarre dream in these muzak-filled halls. Rorie smoothed down her clothes, her hair. She cleared her throat. 'Mr and Mrs Jones?'

'Mr and Mrs Jones' looked up from their work; cool, dispassionate. Vacant. Not only were they unable to recognise her as their daughter, but crucially, because of the Frances disguise, they didn't connect her with the 'lunatic' who had approached them before.

Again, Rorie felt a searing pain shoot through her. She faltered for a moment, catching her breath, then held out her hand. 'I'm Frances Chance,' she began – again using Frances' knowledge to fill in the blanks. 'Tyra Spinorba's assistant? We've met before.'

This is too weird! a voice said in her head. *This is Mum and Dad!*

'Ah, yes,' said Mr Jones. He did a slight double take, as if not entirely sure this was the same Frances Chance he had seen on other occasions. 'Are we needed for something?'

'Yes,' said Rorie-as-Frances. 'And I'm afraid it's urgent. Can you please come straight away?'

'Oh, all right,' said Mr Jones, and shut down his machine; Mrs Jones did likewise.

As the two Joneses obediently followed the Frances-type person, trying to keep up with her brisk pace that was little short of a run, the other workers barely gave them a second glance.

'What's for supper tonight, dear?' Rorie heard Mr Jones say as they went along.

'Fish,' said Mrs Jones.

'That's nice,' said her husband. 'I do like a nice bit of fish.'

Rorie, still in a state of shock over her parents' transformation, could barely believe what she was hearing. The real Mum and Dad never talked like that! They were forever cracking jokes or going off at odd tangents and telling fascinating stories, so that 'fish for supper' might then go on to involve an anecdote about a fish Dad's friend Al once caught, followed by some other Al-related story, possibly involving escapades in Peru or somewhere, then onto a discussion about a Peruvian inventor Mum had met...and on and on, in myriad directions. To hear these very same people diminished to such banality brought tears to Rorie's eyes.

'What about you, Miss Chance?' asked the man who wasn't Dad.

'I'm sorry?'

'Do you like fish?'

Rorie could barely speak through the lump in her throat. 'Um…not especially.'

'Ah.'

'I'm sorry, I'll have to ask you to hurry,' said Rorie, her voice dissolving at the end.

'Are you all right, miss?' asked the woman who was not Mum.

Rorie sniffed loudly. 'Yes, of course. It's just that it's…kind of an emergency.'

'Oh!' Mrs Jones sounded alarmed.

'But there's nothing to worry about,' Rorie added. 'Everything's going to be all right.' She had to positively force the words out, and not let them dissolve again. How many times in the course of Rorie's life had this very woman hushed her and held her, and told her that everything was going to be all right? There had been that night all those years ago, just before her first day at big school – 'Just you wait and see, darling,' Mum had said, smoothing her brow. 'As soon as you see your friends, everything will be all right.' And when Rorie had gone into hospital to have her appendix out, Mum had stuffed Rorie's teddy into her arms. 'There's nothing to be afraid of,' she'd assured her. 'Everything's going to be all right.'

And now, here was that same woman: little more than a zombie.

And here was Rorie, telling *her* it would be all right, when she really, really had no idea what she was going to do next...

Chapter 22
Override

'Where've you *been*?' demanded Elsie, as Rorie emerged from the secret passageway into Room Five.

Rorie barely had time to register her surroundings – though a very odd-looking computer of some sort dominated the room. And there was a familiarity about it... 'I'm sorry Elsie, I had to—'

'Mum! Dad!' cried Elsie, as the figures of Mr and Mrs Jones appeared.

Mr and Mrs Jones stared blankly at her. Rorie stepped forwards. 'Else, remember I explained to you that—'

'Mummeee!' howled Elsie, oblivious as she hurtled towards Mrs Jones and flung her arms around her waist.

Mrs Jones, of course, looked flabbergasted. 'I don't understand...there was another girl, only the other day, and—'

'Yes, I know,' said Rorie, throwing every last ounce of effort into seeming to be Frances. 'We heard about that...excuse me.' She reached over to the still howling Elsie, and gently pulled on her arm. 'Elsie, listen to me. I know it's hard, but...we're not there yet. Elsie? Come on, we haven't got much time.'

'Mummeee! Daddeee!' wailed Elsie.

'Elsie, you're in danger of undoing everything we've achieved so far,' warned Rorie, now taking on a much sterner tone of voice. She was conscious of having to speak in the vaguest possible terms – it was incredibly frustrating that she couldn't just yell, 'Tyra and the rest of them could storm in here any minute, and then we'll be done for!' And she was only too aware that not only were the monkeys probably under control by now, but that Elsie's wails may have been heard – even more acutely aware a moment later, when a pounding noise came at the door leading to the Hex. This did at least have the effect of quietening down Elsie.

'What *is* going on?' demanded Mr Jones, now clearly ruffled himself.

Rorie glanced anxiously at the door. 'It's...no need for alarm, but there's been a malfunction,' she said at last, as some sort of explanation began to form in her head – with the assistance of 'Frances'. 'As you can see, there has been some confusion among a few of the younger members of the community,' she said, impressed at just how Frances-like she sounded. She found that as long as she didn't look 'Mr and Mrs Jones' in the eye, she could pretend that they weren't her parents, and avoid cracking up herself. She had to inhabit Frances as fully as possible – which she hated doing, as it made her feel like she was being swallowed up by her.

'Please disregard the banging on the door,' she continued. 'This is because staff are attempting to get one particularly unruly adolescent under control upstairs. This will require some...' Rorie stared at the bizarre-looking computer, in the hope of kick-starting some Frances associations. And suddenly everything fell into place. That sense of familiarity was coming from the 'Frances' part of her – the part which also knew that Frances had conducted some important operations right here, in this very room...

'Require some...?' prompted Mr Jones.

'...Cerebral adjustments,' were the words that popped out of Rorie's mouth – even though she didn't really know what she meant by it. She thought she'd heard the word 'cerebral' before somewhere, but where?

'Could you please just explain why you need *us*

here?' requested Mrs Jones politely – though there was a tone of impatience coming through.

Rorie stared at her – but not at those eyes that were *so* like her own it made her ache inside... She looked at every part of her *but* her eyes, thinking *Julia Jones, Julia Jones*, as if from Frances' point of view...

It was all coming together now. She knew that this computer was capable of things no other computer could do...and she knew it had been used on 'Mr and Mrs Jones'. And suddenly, she had some idea of what she would have to do to reverse that. As for explaining to the Joneses... Somehow she managed to buy time by filling it with some vaguely convincing-sounding waffle.

'Why I need you here? Ah, yes, well, I was coming to that,' she said, as she began powering up the massive machine. 'You see, there's a necessity every once in a while – and it happens with every department – to...'

Rorie trailed off again, overwhelmed by all the thoughts that were crowding her brain. The machine was unlike any computer she had ever seen before. Its curved black face had six screens, arranged three across the top, then two below that, and one below that. As she sat between the two arms of controls that jutted out either side of her seat, her brain was now deluged with instructions about what to do.

Mr Jones prompted her again. 'To what?'

The door was now being attacked with something more substantial. It wouldn't be long now...

The screens sprang to life before Rorie's eyes, stimulating the Frances part of her brain. 'To make adjustments to some key members of personnel, such as yourselves,' she said, hardly knowing what she was saying. She could feel the Rorie part of her receding. Meanwhile these hands – these bony little Frances-hands with calloused, reddened knuckles – just went on programming in data, and watching the various pieces of information come up on the screens. 'You've complied with us in this kind of procedure before,' she said, not taking her eyes off the screens.

'Yes,' nodded the Joneses in unison.

'Good. This won't take long. Please be seated.'

The Joneses obediently sat down behind her.

'Rorie, what's happening?' asked Elsie, sounding afraid.

'We're going to fix all the stuff that went wrong,' Rorie-as-Frances calmly assured her. 'Everything's going to be fine. But I just need to – before I do anything with Mr and Mrs Jones, something's got to be done about that banging at the door. If I could just call a halt to it somehow…'

'Well, of course you can!' exclaimed Elsie. 'This is *the* computer, right? Tyra's secret one, that's in charge of everything? There must be a way! Just look at what you did when you found that other one on Minimerica, at the Bix house!'

Rorie chewed her lip. 'That was different. All I had to do there was make adjustments to the stuff they pumped into the air, and to the little flashing messages on the billboards. That made it easy to control people. There's none of that here… Oh! But hang on, there might just be another way…' She broke off as she thought hard; only now did she remember something she had noticed about one of the men, when she had been putting on her 'crazy' act. So much had been going on then and since, she had barely had the chance to register it. But as the guard had been attempting to restrain her, she'd spotted a small tattoo behind his ear: a spider tattoo. Exactly the same as Nolita's. Which meant he had been microchipped. Did that mean the same was true of all Tyra's henchmen?

'OK, I think I might be able to fix something here.'

'You better!' remarked Elsie. Still Mr and Mrs Jones sat in their chairs, docile as sheep.

The Frances part of her brain guiding her, Rorie

found her way into 'Staff Modification', and from there to 'Guardsmen'. Yes! Here she could download information to them, either individually or collectively. The collective instructions were, Rorie knew, only ever very general; always along the lines of, 'Go to nearest exit', or 'Gather in the Hex'. But – and here she was suddenly inspired – what if she sent them multiple instructions, all at once?

'Brilliant! This ought to do it,' she said as she collected about a dozen different instructions, then sent them all out. 'I've overloaded the guards,' she explained to Elsie. 'Any minute now, they'll be wandering around like malfunctioning toys, going round in circles and bashing into each other.'

'Oh, cool.'

But the computer said no:

Instructions cannot be carried out. Will disorient the staff.

'I know! That's what I want!' cried Rorie, exasperated.

Still there was the pounding on the door.

'What's the matter?' asked Mr Jones.

'Nothing, nothing,' replied Rorie in a clipped voice. There *was* a way to override this, she was sure…but it was going to take a bit of hunting around.

Bang, bang! That door was going to collapse any second now...

Rorie felt as if her brain might explode at any moment, but she kept on searching. Yes! Here it was:

Override.

The pounding stopped.

'You did it!' cried Elsie.

'All right, sshh!' said Rorie, wiping her brow with relief. She turned her attention to Mr and Mrs Jones, but then paused again. 'Hang on.'

'What is it now?' asked Elsie impatiently.

Rorie stared at the screen, thinking. 'Something else needs fixing...' Tyra, Frances and Dr Visp were still out there. Even with malfunctioning guards wreaking havoc around them, they might be able to break the door down. That was when Rorie had another, even better, idea. Quickly, she chose the names of just two of the men. She cancelled the previous instructions, and quickly replaced them with 'Attack Tyra Spinorba'. Then, for good measure, she instructed two more to 'Lock up Frances Chance and Dr Visp'.

Overriding the computer's objections, Rorie was at last free to apply herself to the most challenging task of all: bringing the two cardboard cut-out versions of Mum and Dad back to life.

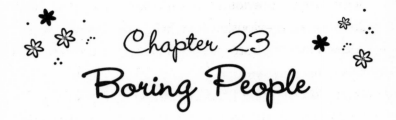

Chapter 23
Boring People

The big black machine had four identical attachments on either side, extending like great long arms. These now mobilised. Guiding them as she sat in front of the multiple screens, Rorie was aware that the thing resembled a huge spider. Two of the arms looped overhead, and moved towards the heads of Mr and Mrs Jones, one to each.

'Oh, Rorie, I'm scared!' cried Elsie.

'No!' snapped Rorie, still studying the information in front of her. 'You mustn't interrupt now, Elsie. It could be very dangerous. You just have to trust me.'

The arms that were now in contact with the Joneses' heads corresponded to the two screens in the middle, and they filled with information about them. Pictures, history…and background.

'There they are!' squealed Elsie. 'That's them!'

Rorie too felt an indescribable thrill at seeing it confirmed for her on the screen:

James Jones, previously Arran Silk.

Julia Jones, previously Laura Silk.

Meanwhile the bottom screen described the actions of the arms:

Probe locating and preparing trepanation area.

Cascading blobs indicated time needed for this.

'What's happening, Rorie?' demanded Elsie.

'Well, I think...um,' Rorie struggled to put into words what she understood from Frances. 'They're having a kind of...well, a sort of operation.'

'Operation?!' cried Elsie. 'But is it safe?'

'Oh, yes,' Rorie assured her. 'It's...Elsie, I'd rather not think about it, but from what I understand, there's some sort of groundwork that was done before, and it's just a case of – well, er...unplugging.' She couldn't help grimacing at this word.

Elsie didn't like the sound of it either. 'Eurgh! Doesn't it hurt?'

'No, that area of the scalp is sealed off, and we don't have any feelings in our brains.'

'Really?'

'Uh-huh.'

Location and preparation successful, announced the

computer. **Enter arachnoid mater?**

'*Yes*,' responded Rorie blankly.

The middle screens displayed graphics of what was happening. As Frances, Rorie understood that the 'trepanation area' referred to a tiny hole in each of the Joneses' skulls, no more than a millimetre in diameter, and 'arachnoid mater' was a layer of tissue surrounding the brain. She regarded the whole thing dispassionately, as if she were watching it in a movie.

Contact with arachnoid mater established.

Now was the moment of truth; this was the point at which she could do something. The screens were running through dozens of images per second from each of Mr and Mrs Jones.

'Now what's happening?' asked Elsie.

'The computer's downloading memories of every experience they've had since they were last connected,' Rorie explained, as images of everything, from working the machines to eating their lunch or relaxing at home, appeared. In fact, their memories seemed to consist mostly of those three things. All their leisure time appeared to be spent on the Shenham residential complex.

'Wow. They've had the boringest time,' remarked Elsie. 'How can they stand it?'

'*Because* they've had their heads messed with,' explained Rorie, exasperated. 'I thought that was obvious!'

Then there were the faces of people, and whole subsets of random associations with each of them. There were hopes, fears, challenges...all of the most mundane variety. Eventually the images slowed down, and came to a halt altogether. 'That's it,' said Rorie. 'That's all of the past fourteen weeks of their lives, sucked out of them and squished into the computer.'

'Really?' gasped Elsie.

'I know, unbelievable, isn't it? I reckon Tyra's got something here no one else in the world has.'

'It's *evil*.'

'That's an understatement... OK, now to get the real Mum and Dad back – oh no, hang on.' Rorie scrunched her eyes tight shut and gripped her temples as she focused hard on the Frances-knowledge.

'What?' shrieked Elsie. 'Can't you do it?'

'No, it's not that, it's...' Rorie swivelled back to face the computer and sprang into action. 'There's other stuff to get out first.' As she punched out a sequence of commands, she explained to Elsie. 'Here: surrogate memories. We've got to get these out – they're the fake memories installed by Rexco. My

God, just look at them! To think I nearly left them in.'

On the screens, small children played with blocks, frolicked in the park, petted dogs. The images speeded up, and schooldays came and went in a blur…adolescence passed without incident – clearly 'James and Julia Jones' never rebelled against anything. James met Julia and vice versa; all the rites of passage were present and correct, lined up with all the dull predictability of a row of frozen meals in a supermarket. The Joneses were like a pair of two-dimensional characters from one of those create-a-family computer games, invented by someone with no imagination at all.

At last the fake history was fully transferred. 'Right, that's got rid of that rubbish!' declared Rorie. 'Now for the really important part: retrieving their *real* memories.'

Elsie shut her eyes and clasped her hands to her heart. 'Oh, *yes*.'

'OK, I need complete silence for this.' Rorie tried to focus every last drop of thought on locating the right files – *all* of them. To miss anything out could be disastrous. And yet, even as she tried to apply herself to the task, something was holding her back. Again she held her head in her hands. 'Oh!' she wailed.

'What's the matter?' asked Elsie.

'I can't...it's not coming!'

'Oh, but it has to!' cried Elsie. 'Come on, Rorie, you can do it!'

'Yes, I know I can...I mean, I did the last bit, but...oh!'

'Mr and Mrs Jones' still sat in their seats, immobile, empty vessels, ready for filling.

Elsie jumped up and down. 'Rorie, come *on*. Remember the tiger-lilies.'

Rorie gazed blankly at her; her mind was so befuddled right now, she didn't even understand what Elsie was talking about.

'The tiger-lilies, the *story*,' Elsie pressed. 'How they picked up the king and shook him, until he was so freaked out he ran away, and then all the fairies were free, and the flowers in the garden got to be the colours they wanted to be.'

'Oh. Right.' Rorie sighed heavily. 'Else, that's all very well, but it's not *inspiration* I need right now: it's not as if I don't want to do this. It's that I'm, I'm...'

'Scared?'

Rorie broke down. 'All right, yes! I'm scared, Elsie. I'm *terrified*. You don't know what it's like to be changed like this—'

'Well, I might've found out if they'd done that 'speriment on me,' Elsie remarked wistfully. Part of her wished it had happened, and she had at last discovered what it was like to change as if by magic, like Rorie could.

'Thank God they didn't!' said Rorie. 'Look, when I'm just talking to you like this, it's almost like I'm me. But when I'm doing the Frances stuff, it's different; I *inhabit* her. She kind of takes over – except that I'm still governed by my own will. But...never mind sailing boats, flying planes – this is the hardest thing I've yet had to do, because...' Rorie thought for a moment. 'Because Frances herself isn't all that well practised at it. I think...I think Tyra was involved, too; there may be missing links in the process. And I don't have anything of Tyra's to help me. Do you see?'

Elsie looked desperate. 'Well, what do we *do*, then?'

'That's what scares me. I have to lose myself to Frances even more. Only then can I hope to pull this off. There's always a level of resistance, you see; I need to kind of switch that off. Do you understand? But...what if I *really* lose myself? For good? I'm already scared after what happened last time. Or, what if I do that, and then Frances' motivation takes over? And then she'd wreck everything.'

'Really?'

'Well, think about it. It's possible, isn't it?'

'But you'll never know if you don't try.'

'I know. But I'm *scared*.'

'Well, you mustn't be. You can't. Like I said, you got to be like the tiger-lilies.'

'Elsie—'

'I mean, *brave* like them. Wearing tiger stripes, *being* like a tiger. Would a tiger be scared right now?'

Rorie didn't have the heart to point out that a tiger was hardly capable of the sort of complex rational thought that was required here. But the reminder of the story made her turn and look at 'Mrs Jones' – that poor wax model of the real-life, vibrant person who had sat on her bed and shared such amazing tales with her. 'I guess not, Elsie,' said Rorie at last. 'And neither would Mum have been.'

'Don't talk about her like that,' snapped Elsie. 'She's not dead, you know!'

Suddenly, Rorie felt a surge of fire through her veins. 'No, you're right. And neither's Dad. She turned back to the computer. 'OK. I'm ready.'

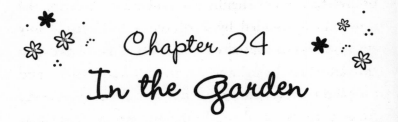

Chapter 24
In the Garden

I am Frances, I am Frances. My name is Frances Chance, and I work for Tyra Spinorba, head of Rexco...

So went the mantra inside Rorie's head, over and over. She could almost feel the 'Rorie' part of her shrinking away; she forced herself to embrace that process. No longer could she worry about whether she would get herself back. This was her only chance of restoring Mum and Dad to their former selves – not only that, but she might just succeed in bringing down Tyra Spinorba as well, along with all those Tramlawn schools like Poker Bute Hall...and maybe even Minimerica, and every other piece of the global Rexco web.

OK...where did I put all that stuff? she asked herself. Those parcels of memories that had been sucked out of Arran and Laura Silk were well hidden, that much she knew. Even if there were ever some sort of investigation at Shenham – unlikely, considering the power now wielded by Zedforce – and even if any suspicion were roused over the resemblance between 'Mr and Mrs Jones' and Arran and Laura Silk...and even if an investigator were to bypass interrogating the Joneses themselves and somehow *know* that their identities had been sucked away into this computer, itself pretty well hidden – well, Tyra Spinorba had well and truly made sure that this material would not be easy to find.

It was not even easy for 'Frances' herself to find. The new hybrid Francesrorie that Rorie had become now realised that she could only access it by going into virtual reality mode. Yet another journey. 'Hang in there,' she just about managed to tell Elsie, before pressing the button that sent forth two more of the machine's arms, this time towards her own head.

'Rorie, I'm scared!' she heard.

'It's all right. Think of the...of the...' Rorie was so immersed in Frances now, it was almost as if her recent conversation with Elsie hadn't taken place.

'The tiger-lilies?' came the little voice.

'That's right,' said Francesrorie, as two semicircular bands now extended from the computer arms, and clamped themselves onto her head. 'The tiger-lilies...'

Boom. All around her was clear blue sky – below her, too. But that didn't matter, as she was able to fly. She soared over a beautiful, sparkling city – but she didn't descend there. That was not the place, she knew.

She flew on.

A mountain range reared up: snow-topped peaks glistened in the sunlight. Francesrorie carried on. Should she go straight, or left, or right? *To the west*, said the voice in her head. The west looked bleak, but this was the way; yes, this was the way. But she was slowing down. Why was she slowing down? She consulted the energy meter, which hung in the air just above her sightline: it was low. Already? She would need to pick up some sustenance – but where? Nothing but barren land. She would simply have to keep going. Then, at last, woodland: here she would find food! Francesrorie swooped down among the trees. Yes: here was a mouse, recently killed. That would do. She rested for a moment, absorbing the 'nutrients' from the gigantic creature (so much larger than a normal mouse!) until her energy level was replenished, then off she flew again.

On and on, through the woods. Something told her she wouldn't find what she was looking for here. She rose back up, above the trees. On and on, and now the woodland gave way to suburban houses and parkland. It was the park she needed to head for – but now she realised the light was failing. She hadn't noticed the shadows lengthening; the sun was going down – and fast. Much faster than usual. This, like the energy drain, was another trap. Once the sun went down, she knew, it would be twelve hours before she would have another chance to locate the data. Time was really running out now. *Head for the house*, the voice said. *There's a house somewhere in the grounds of this park.*

Longer and longer shadows; but here was a bandstand beside a lake, and the house – yes, there was the house, at the top of the rise. And beside it, a flower garden. Yes! This was the place. But dusk was approaching... There was one special kind of flower she needed to find. Which was...what? A rose? A geranium? No...some other flower, one that was golden in colour, and associated with a cat of some sort – a big, golden cat. A lion? No, no...a tiger! The *tiger-lilies*, that was where she had to go. She zoomed over to the star-shaped flowers, their gold now tarnished with shade. And here was the one, right in the middle of the flowerbed; this was the one. Francesrorie hurtled towards it...

Then stopped, suspended in midair.

She pushed and strained, but she could get no further. It took a moment to realise why. Then, as her limbs flailed around, she saw that it was because she was a fly, and she was caught in a spider's web. She was stuck, just millimetres from her goal...and the sun was about to set.

Now she was being thrown up and down, side to side, lurching like a bucking-bronco rider, yet stuck as firmly to the web as if her feet were in hardened concrete.

A massive black spider was edging down the web towards her.

Chapter 25
Black Widow

Had she been anyone else but Francesrorie, she would have given up at this point. But she knew that the spider represented Tyra Spinorba, and that all she wanted from her was some information.

'Name?' the spider demanded.

'Frances Chance,' responded the fly, undeterred.

The spider inched closer and arched her two front legs threateningly at her. 'Password?'

Francesrorie was filled with revulsion. 'Black widow,' she managed.

The spider's mouthparts dripped with glutinous acid, ready for attack. 'Birth date of subject number one?'

Francesrorie felt quite sick with fear, and although she knew that 'subject number one' was Arran Silk, for a moment she could not for the life of her think what his date of birth was. Then, after a stomach-churning moment or two, it popped into her head; she gave it. The spider sat there, hovering. Surely now it would let her pass? It *was* right, she was sure of it. Francesrorie tried to step forwards, but still she was stuck.

'One moment,' said the spider, its six eyes glaring down at her. The disgusting mouthparts flexed themselves in anticipation. Oh, how revolting it was! 'Location of data: explain the choice.'

'Explain the choice?' repeated Francesrorie. 'What does that mean?' Now her entire field of vision was taken up with that horrible six-eyed face, with its acid-dripping mouth tube.

'Location of data,' the spider repeated. 'Explain the choice.'

Francesrorie flew into a panic. 'Look, I don't understand! Come on, I've answered three security questions, surely that's enough!'

'Extra security question must be answered!'

The sun was dipping below the horizon; only seconds left now.

'I...oh, hang on: you mean the flower! It's the flower, isn't it? Why a tiger-lily? Is that what you mean by "explain the choice"?'

The spider said nothing. The sun dipped lower; less than half of it was visible now.

That *had* to be what it meant. 'OK, the tiger-lily…it comes from a story invented by subject number two. As well as being a bedtime story she used to tell her daughters, it was…it was…' There was some other part to this answer, she knew. That is, the 'Frances' bit of her knew. She thought so hard, it felt as if her brain might burst. Then a flash of inspiration. 'It was the codename she and subject number one gave to their last Smart clothing project.'

Whoosh! The spider and its web were gone. From the centre of the golden flower, great big juicy droplets began to spurt forth. As they did so, they blew themselves up into bubbles that hovered all around her. She knew that at last she had found what she was looking for, and could now go back to the real world…

'Rorie? Are you back?' came Elsie's voice.

'Um…yeah,' said Francesrorie, steadying herself as the clamps eased away from her head. She was feeling quite woozy. 'OK, I have located the material,' she added in a typical Frances monotone. On some other level, she was aware of how absurdly inadequate a term this was for what she had just done. She had rescued all the memories that made Mum and Dad who they were…and managed to make it sound like finding a piece of paper. Meanwhile the bubbles hung there on the screens in front of her. She delivered the necessary commands, and now, two at a time, the bubbles exploded their contents onto the middle screens, dozens of images per second, representing information as it hurtled at lightning speed from the machine into the arachnoid mater of the brains of her parents.

A whole lifetime of memories. And these, unlike those of the Joneses, were rich and varied, with all the colour and fragrance of a spice market, all the intricate complexity of a Persian carpet, all the wondrous glory of the stars.

And, most crucially, there were their memories of Rorie and Elsie, from birth right through to that last day, as they got ready to head out for their meeting with Rexco.

'There's you!' cried Elsie, as soon as the little baby became recognisable. 'And me…hey, I remember that! And that…oh, it's all here, it's amazing!'

As the images slowed down, Francesrorie knew there was still one last thing she had to do. 'There's still the ideas,' she told Elsie. 'Tyra has been…growing them.'

Elsie frowned. '*Growing* them?'

Saying nothing more, Francesrorie plunged once again into virtual reality mode. This time she didn't need to answer any security questions; it was all there for the taking. Only because she was who she was did she know to look in the first place. In another part of the garden, she found two young saplings. She dug away at their roots with her bare hands – glad to find that this time she *had* hands – until she got right down to the acorns from which they had been grown. Then she took the acorns and set them free, throwing them up into the air, where they simply hovered, lightly buffeted by the breeze…

'This is the stuff,' she told Elsie, as she indicated the acorns on the screens, back in the real world. 'The ideas; the inventions. Tyra has had this computer programmed to take them and develop them in…let's say, new directions.'

'The shapeshifting?'

'Exactly. But whereas the computer can generate theories, it can't experiment with putting the ideas into practice. That's where the girls came in.'

'The girls?'

'Rorie and Elsie.'

'Yes, Rorie – you and me!'

Francesrorie gave Elsie a blank look, half-frowned,

then turned back to the screens. 'Now we just need to move these acorns back...' Ignoring the noises Elsie was making (what *was* she making such a fuss about?) she punched out another command, and up came multiple images of the DNA double helix, cells, fibres, clothing... When it had all been transferred, she instructed the machine to disengage. The two arms slowly came away from the heads of the two subjects.

'Now we just need to wait,' she said, turning around. 'It takes a few minutes for everything to settle down.'

But now a different sound was coming from the door to the Hex – that of a chainsaw.

Elsie's face was filled with terror. 'But we haven't *got* a few minutes! And what's more,' – she grabbed hold of the cardigan Rorie was wearing, and yanked at it – 'you're done now, take this off!'

'Oh, OK,' said Francesrorie passively. Her eyelids drooped, she yawned. 'Oh, I'm so tired!'

'This is no time to be tired, Rorie! We still haven't got out of here. How the heck we gonna do that?'

'Um...well, through there, I suppose.' She pointed to the other door, the one that led to the secret passage. She yawned again, apparently oblivious to the chainsaw that was now visible at the Hex entrance. 'In a while...'

Elsie gave her a big smack on the face.

'Hey! What was that for?'

'You gotta wake up, Rorie! We need to excape! And you're *Rorie*, OK? Rorie Silk, and I'm your sister, and—'

'Elsie? What are you doing here?'

The two girls turned and looked. The woman – Mrs Jones, Mrs Stemphior, Laura Silk – was regarding Elsie crossly, hands on hips.

Elsie was dumbfounded.

'Did you sneak into the back of the car?' said the woman. 'No, hang on, I distinctly remember dropping you off at school...Arran? What's Elsie doing here?'

Elsie squealed with more-than-delight, and threw herself at her. 'Mummy! Oh, it's *worked*, Rorie. It's really worked!'

Chapter 26
Avatar Army

'The little scamp! Elsie, you're a terror,' said Dad – though he couldn't stop a smile from creeping over his face. 'How did you manage to get in here without us even...' He paused, distracted by the loud grinding noise of the chainsaw. 'Hey, what's going on?'

Elsie smeared the tears from her face and unclamped herself from his leg. 'Tell you later. But we're in *danger*, c'mon!' She took him by the wrist and pulled, straining in the direction of the other door.

Mum stood up, holding her head. 'I feel weird. Something feels...not right.'

'That's 'cause it isn't!' cried Elsie. 'C'mon! We gotta get away from here!'

'And who are you?' asked Mum, addressing Rorie.

'It's Rorie,' said Elsie. 'I know she looks different but she'll change...oh, I can't 'splain, we got to go, all of us!' She tried desperately to pull on all three of them in turn, but she was one tiny person and they were three big, heavy people who were also very confused.

But soon Dad sensed the danger as well. He frowned and rubbed at his hair in his familiar Dad way. 'You're right, Lols,' he said to Mum. 'This is…can't put my finger on it, but…yeah, maybe we should…'

'Yes!' cried Elsie. 'Oh, come *on*, Rorie,' she urged, as she tugged on her drowsy sister's arm.

'OK,' said Rorie, stumbling after her. 'I'm Rorie,' she muttered to herself. 'I'm *Rorie*…'

They got through the door to the passage just as their pursuers broke into the computer room. Dad, now apparently understanding that they must not be caught, even if he was a bit vague on the specifics, slammed the door shut behind them, then picked up Elsie and ran. Mum and Rorie did their best to keep up.

Still half-Frances, and very disoriented indeed, Rorie was nevertheless filled with a strange sense that something wonderful had happened – though she wasn't quite sure what it was. It was as if she had entered some sort of no-man's-land between 'Frances' and 'Rorie', neither one nor the other. But on some level she knew that these people were very important to her, and she mustn't part from them.

They ran down the corridor, then came to the secret entrance to the main passageway. She watched as the man, together with this little girl called Elsie, instinctively pushed, and the door slid aside. 'That way!' cried Elsie, indicating the direction of the factory. All was clear until they were almost at the doors to the factory. Then two guards burst through, and hurtled towards them. But no sooner were the men there than they began whirling around in circles. One of them fell over, and seemed unable to figure out how to get up, while the other went back through the doors.

'Don't worry about them,' said Elsie proudly. 'Rorie fixed it so they're useless.'

But behind them, whoever it was that had broken into the computer room was now gaining on them fast.

On the factory floor, they battled their way through the line of workers, who had apparently formed a queue when the alarm went off, and were still quietly standing there, awaiting instructions for what they were supposed to do next. Rorie, although confused, was still as desperate as the rest of her little group to get away. The adrenaline was pumping now, edging out the crippling tiredness that had been threatening to overwhelm her. Not daring to look back, she threw herself up the stairs and out through the emergency exit, closely followed by the woman, the man and Elsie. Dashing across the broad lawns surrounding the complex, it seemed they were at last free. It felt wonderful to Rorie to be out in the brilliant sunshine of a glorious summer's day; it felt as if she had been enclosed in darkness for years...

Something caught at her ankle. She reached down to free it, but some sort of fine silken thread appeared from nowhere and wrapped itself around her arm. 'Hey!' she cried, and tried to tug herself free. More and more threads came forth. She looked around, and saw that the same thing was happening to the others.

'Help!' cried Elsie. 'We're being cocooned, just like I was when we first got here!'

Rorie searched her memory; yes, there was an image there of this same little girl struggling to escape from a web of silk. It felt as if it had been a very long time ago, in some other lifetime...but maybe it was just that an awful lot that had happened since then.

The others were thrashing around frantically. 'Aagh, what is this stuff?' gasped the woman.

Even the man couldn't free himself. 'I can't

believe how strong it is. Damn! They're getting close…whoever they are.'

Rorie turned to see several figures advancing from the building. 'They're Tyra's avatars,' she found herself saying – though she hadn't the faintest idea why, or what she meant by it. The words had simply popped into her head.

'Oh, no – you're right,' said Elsie.

Meanwhile, layer upon layer of silken mesh was building up around each of them. Daylight was reduced to little pinholes, through which Rorie was now aware of cars arriving, and flashing lights. Her first thought was, *The police! Thank heavens, we're rescued!* But then she recognised the purple and silver cars and realised that no, they weren't rescued: this was Zedforce.

Now they were virtually surrounded by vehicles, and officers were piling out – whole legions of them. Meanwhile, the army of Tyras was advancing from behind. At least two dozen in number, they strode forwards, a row of identical moon-faces. Blankly serene, with that characteristic half-smile; even now they still appeared strangely benevolent. Younger-looking than Tyra herself, they were united in their single-minded purpose.

Still Rorie struggled, but it was hopeless. The silk cocoon was stretchy, but incredibly strong. Then a slackening; something – a laser device? – was cutting through the stuff. A huge hole opened up. No sooner was she released than two Zedforce officers were upon her, clamping her in handcuffs.

The familiar *phut-phut-phut* sound of a helicopter made her look up. *Oh, no, not again.* 'Why d'you need to airlift in even *more* men?' she yelled over the noise. 'There's only four of us, for heaven's sake!'

But the reaction she got was not what she expected. Her captors, along with many of the other Zedforce officers, gazed up at the skies. Many seemed to be discussing the situation with a sense of urgency, their clothes flapping in the wind created by the rotor blades. The avatars, however, just kept on coming, apparently oblivious.

A higher-ranking Zedforce officer approached the captors and said something to them that Rorie couldn't hear over the din. Then she was swiftly pulled away, along with the others, as the rest of the officers beat a hasty retreat to their vehicles.

'Give up your captives!' an amplified voice commanded from the nearest helicopter, as a long rope ladder descended from it. 'We're filming this whole thing as evidence!'

There was mass confusion among the Zedforce men, but the avatars were still undeterred. Nothing and nobody was going to come between them and their objective, and now they all simultaneously reached for what looked horribly like gun holsters...

Suddenly there was a loud shushing noise and everything went fuzzy. The next moment Rorie felt an intense, searing sting in her eyes. 'Aagh!' she cried, clamping her hands over them. At the same time, she felt the grip on her arms loosen.

'Over here, Rorie!' came a strange, hollow-sounding voice from the darkness. Now she felt another hand grab her by the arm, as the others slipped away. 'It's OK, it's just tear gas,' said the voice. 'It's me, Moll.'

Rorie tried to respond, but all she could do was cough, and her nose was streaming. 'Quick!' commanded the strange Moll-voice. 'You won't be able to open your eyes, but you're gonna have to put your hands on the ladder...that's it...come on, good!'

Rorie felt like a blind, mewling kitten as she struggled to climb the ladder. The noise was impossibly loud, and the ladder lurched about crazily, but she was determined. 'Elshie...' she garbled, unable to look around for the little girl.

'It's all right, Elsie's coming. And your mum and dad.'

'Mum'n'Dad...oh!' Rorie felt a huge sob well up inside her. 'Mum and Dad!'

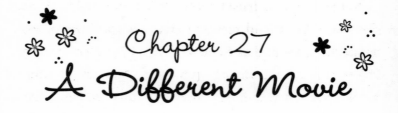

Chapter 27
A Different Movie

It was just the shock she'd needed. Everything came flooding back as she sat there in pain, eyes closing out all light, nothing but darkness and noise all around her.

'Rorie! Is that you?' cried Dad, having heard her voice. 'Where did you spring from?'

'I...uh...' Rorie's voice cracked up with emotion.

'I'd better leave you four together,' said the other voice – the one belonging to Moll.

'Moll! It really is you,' said Rorie. 'Now you sound like yourself.'

'That's 'cause I took off the respirator. I'm sorry, there just wouldn't have been time to supply you with them as well. But don't worry, I know the tear gas stings, but you'll be fine. Any minute now, it'll wear off. OK, I'm going. You guys have a lot to catch up on.'

'But...Moll!' called Rorie.

'Later,' came the Moll-voice. 'Later.'

Rorie listened, frustrated in her blind isolation as she heard her friend retreat to the cockpit. Questions nagged at her mind as to how Moll had got away from Poker Bute Hall, how the rescue had come about...but more than anything, she was still dealing with her sheer joy and amazement that here, really and truly, after all this time, were Mum and Dad!

Then came the sensation of rising up as the helicopter headed off, taking them up and away to a new phase in their lives. And in the new phase she was, again, *Rorie*. Not Frances, not even Francesrorie, and certainly not any of the other incarnations she'd been through either. Just Rorie, soaring up into a new beginning.

As promised, the stinging in her eyes subsided. Tentatively, Rorie opened them, and there they were – real, solid, three-dimensional: Mum and Dad. Now they, too, opened their eyes, blinking and rubbing.

'Oh, I can still hardly believe it!' Rorie burst into tears, and this set Elsie off too.

Mum and Dad just looked on, bemused. They were still under the impression that they had only just seen their daughters that morning, so they had no reason to get choked up with emotion.

For a while, the four of them sat not saying anything, dumbstruck by the shock of it all. Rorie wanted so badly to give Mum and Dad a huge hug, but couldn't as they were all strapped into their seats.

Yes, this really is Mum and Dad! Rorie said to herself over and over. Just to be sure she was back to normal herself, she studied her hands, and felt her hair and face. *Yes, I'm really me!* New tears of relief welled up in her eyes. She didn't even care that the Frances mole still seemed to be there.

Dad, however, was perplexed. 'Hey, what's that mark on your cheek?' he asked.

Rorie's hand instinctively shot up to cover it. 'Oh, it's...nothing.'

Dad was too full of questions to care anyway. 'Well, can you explain to me what the heck went on back there? Because I haven't the faintest idea.'

Rorie was still piecing everything together herself. Now she was remembering all the work she did as Frances on Tyra's master computer, to transform 'James and Julia Jones' back into the real Arran and Laura Silk.

'You haven't the faintest idea,' she said at last, 'because you don't remember anything of the past fourteen weeks of your life.'

Dad frowned. 'Well, of course I do! How could I not? It's been the culmination of all my work.'

'Yes, Rorie, whatever are you talking about?' asked Mum. 'Why would you think he'd have forgotten such a huge chunk of his life?'

'Because I know he has,' said Rorie. 'You have, too.'

'Yeah,' added Elsie. 'You only fink you remember, but there's this whole bit missing.'

Mum looked exasperated. 'What "bit"?'

'Well,' said Elsie, sighing and putting her hands on her hips, the way she did when she was being all grown up. 'Basically, Rexco kidnapped you, 'cause they din't want your invention to get out, 'cause they want people to go on buying lots of cloves for ever and ever—'

'Elsie,' Rorie tried to interject.

'So what they did was they, like, *sucked* all the inventions out of your heads,' Elsie went on, pulling at the air with her hands, 'and *growed* them in the computer so that Tyra Spinorba – she's the boss-lady – could change herself any way she liked, instead of just having atavars—'

'It's *avatars*, Elsie,' Rorie interrupted. 'And slow down! They haven't got a clue what you're on about, and it all sounds completely mad!'

'It's OK, Rorie,' said Mum, smiling. 'She can tell her story if she wants. You know what a wild imagination she has!'

'Yes, but it's not a story!' Rorie retorted. 'It's all true; it's just that it can't be making any sense to you! Look...' She sighed, trying to fathom the best way of dealing with this. 'OK,' she said at last. 'Describe to me what you did yesterday.'

'You know perfectly well!' said Mum. 'We showed you girls our invention, then Dad announced we had a meeting today, so we stayed up late into the night, and...what?'

Rorie was smiling softly and shaking her head. 'That was *three and a half months ago*, Mum. Look outside. See the trees?'

Mum and Dad both leant forwards and peered out of the window. Below them were fields bordered by oak and beech trees – all filled out with lush green, midsummer leaves.

Dad slammed back in his seat, aghast. 'No, it's not possible!'

'It's early March!' cried Mum.

'No, it isn't,' said Rorie, almost feeling guilty for having to put them through this. 'It's *late June*. Take a look at your Shels...if you have them?'

Dad fished in his pocket, took out his Shel and stared at it. 'Hey, this isn't mine! Why've I got somebody else's...no, don't answer that. June 20th! My God, no...this isn't possible!'

'Arran!' cried Mum suddenly, gripping his arm as she jerked up her foot. 'Look at these awful shoes! What the heck am I wearing?'

'They're Julia Jones' shoes,' said Elsie. 'And yeah, they're yuck.'

'That's who you were until less than an hour ago,' explained Rorie. 'You've been...uh, quite literally, in *her* shoes all this time. I mean, not that "Julia Jones" actually exists...'

Mum put her hand to her head again. 'Oh, my head hurts! Well, where on earth have *you* two been these past few months, then?'

Rorie thought she would burst with anticipation as Inspector Dixon stepped ahead and opened the front door.

'The place is pretty much just as you left it,' he explained, as he slid the key into the lock. 'Though I did have someone come in and clean out the fridge.'

Rorie felt Mum's hand grip hers tightly as they entered the house. Dixon had difficulty pushing the door open against the weight of the mail piled up behind it. Finally, they all stepped over the threshold.

Mum ran a finger over the surface of the hall table. 'Oh my God. I feel as if I've been in a time machine.' She turned to the girls. 'You've no idea...to me, I was just *here*. Only yesterday! And yet...' She sighed and shook her head.

Rorie and Elsie had done their best to explain everything that had happened, both to their parents and to themselves – although missing out the part about Arthur Clarkson, the lightning strike, and Rorie's subsequent chameleon powers. Elsie had almost let that one slip, but Rorie had talked over her loudly, and managed to divert the conversation. And when Mum asked who had been looking after Arthur Clarkson all this time, Rorie had lied: 'He's with Maya next door.' She hoped Mum and Dad hadn't noticed the sharp dig in the ribs she gave Elsie to keep her quiet. It could wait until later; Mum and Dad were devastated enough as it was by everything else.

And they were *very* upset.

They were also shocked to hear about Poker Bute Hall, and how Dad's own brother had been involved in such a nasty scheme. 'I've never got on with Harris, as you know,' Dad had said. 'But *this*...I never would have imagined it.'

Rorie and Elsie had described how they had ended up at Nolita Newbuck's house ('*The* Nolita Newbuck?' Mum had gasped), and how they had discovered that she was being controlled by Misty. The description of their accidental discovery of Minimerica was the most unbelievable part of all. Some way through it Rorie had simply said, 'Enough! I think we need to stop now.' It was all too much – and the exhaustion from the Frances transformation was beginning to overwhelm her. 'Later,' she'd insisted. 'I'll tell you the rest later.'

'Well, I'll be off then,' said Inspector Dixon. 'Just wanted to see you safely home.'

Mum took his hand in both of hers. 'Thank you *so* much, Inspector. I...I don't know how to thank you enough.' Her chin wobbled, and her voice broke up as tears threatened to overwhelm her once again. His kindness to Rorie and Elsie throughout their troubled time had been much remarked on by the girls. But more than anything, she had been shocked and disturbed by everything the girls had been through.

'Yes, thank you,' said Dad – himself red-eyed from

earlier tears of grief mingled with relief.

'You get some rest, and I'll see you in the morning,' said Dixon.

The door closed behind him.

Dad sighed and picked up a handful of mail. 'You know what, Lols? I feel as if my life is a movie, and I just stepped out to go the loo, and missed a really crucial part of the plot.'

'You do?' said Mum. 'I feel as if I'm in a different movie altogether.'

Chapter 28
Ninety-nine Per Cent

For the first time in months, Rorie woke up in her own bed. She gazed at the back of her bedroom door, which was entirely covered in a collage of photos of herself with friends and pets, and assorted music and netfilm idols. It was so very familiar, and yet...somehow it now felt as if it all belonged to someone else. So much had happened since she was last here that all those people seemed as if they occupied a different universe.

All the same, her heart soared as she thought about Mum and Dad, safely home in the next room. She could hardly believe it, even now. On her way to the bathroom, she couldn't resist taking a peep inside their room, to check they really were there. And yes, there was the reassuring shape of the two bodies, just visible in the gloom. Still fast asleep.

And they were fine; there didn't seem to be any

permanent damage – unless you counted that missing period of fourteen weeks. The family doctor had swiftly been summoned to examine them the previous evening, and was shocked at the story of what had been done to them. 'I'm not aware that the technology is available for such a procedure,' she'd said, doubtfully – but Rorie was backed up by Mum. 'Rorie wouldn't lie about this,' she'd assured her.

Dr Proby had been cautiously optimistic about their condition. 'Well, I'm referring you to a neurologist, just to be sure,' she'd said. 'Physically you seem to be fine—'

'Apart from the holes in our skulls,' Mum had remarked jokingly.

But Dr Proby was unconcerned about that. 'Actually, that's not a problem; it makes no difference to brain function at all.'

'In fact I believe some people think it helps,' said Dad. 'It's called "trepanning", isn't it?'

'That's right,' said Dr Proby. 'And it's been around for centuries – millennia, even. It was once thought to release evil spirits.'

'Ha! Only this time, they did it to let the evil spirits *in*,' remarked Rorie.

Dr Proby dismissed the 'spirit' business as nonsense. Which, of course, it was. But, remembering the fairy-tale version of this whole nightmare that she'd told Elsie as her way of trying to make sense of it all, Rorie was struck by just how much it felt as if Mum and Dad really had been released from a spell cast by some wicked fairy.

Rorie had been reassured by Dr Proby's assessment that Mum and Dad wouldn't need anything else done to them, apart from the removal of the tiny, capped metal tubes that had been inserted into their scalps when they were first operated on; it was through these that Rorie had been able to reverse the process, and their presence had meant that it was a completely clean, painless procedure; the brain, the doctor had confirmed, contained no nerve endings.

Rorie wandered back to bed. She opened the curtains in her room and gazed out onto the dewy, misty jungle the back garden had become, and wondered about Nolita, Luke and all the others still at Kethly Merwiden. Now that Tyra Spinorba was being questioned (made possible because she had indeed been locked up by two of her men, thanks to Rorie's – or possibly Frances' – ingenuity), was this really the beginning of the end for Rexco? Rorie hoped Inspector Dixon would have some good news for them when he returned later that morning...

Dad wandered into the room still shiny from his shower, the last to come down for breakfast.

Elsie threw herself at him. 'Daddeee!'

Dad laughed as he picked her up and hugged her. 'Mmm! My little Fluff!' He twirled her around, then put her down. As he did so, he ended up directly facing Arthur Clarkson's cage. He pulled away the cloth that was covering it. 'Hey, what's Maya keeping Arthur in? We'd better go over and get him back.'

Rorie and Elsie looked at each other. How much to say? Just that poor old Arthur was dead, or…everything else?

But they were saved by the doorbell: it was Inspector Dixon. The girls crowded around him instantly, bombarding him with questions. 'Is there any news? Is Tyra going to prison? What's happening at Kethly Merwiden? Where's Moll?'

'Not a whole lot to report yet,' he said. 'We've got a massive team down at Shenham – though there's also a high Zedforce presence, and we're trying to deal with that. And I'm told Moll should be here any minute… By the way, please don't leave the house for now; I'll make sure you have all you need. I'm just thinking of your security.'

'Oh…OK,' said Dad.

The doorbell rang again. 'Ah, that'll be Moll!'

Rorie jumped up, and dashed over to give her friend a hug. Even though they'd had so little time to get to know each other, it felt now as if they'd been a part of each other's lives for ever.

'I can't stay long,' said Moll. 'Got to head back to the station; my parents are picking me up. Don't worry, I'm not going to be sent back to Poker Bute Hall! But I wanted to come by first and thank you properly…'

'Thank *us*?' said Rorie. '*We're* the ones who should be thanking *you*!'

'The point is, it was you who got me out of there,' explained Moll, as they all went and sat at the kitchen table. 'You sent me that necklace – that's what triggered everything off. If you hadn't done that…well, who knows? I might have just gone on being a zombie for my entire life. My God! To think what I was like! I swear, it's as if I just wasn't me at all – I was a completely different person. You have no idea!'

'Oh, I think I do,' said Rorie. '*Really* I do… Anyway, so what happened? When you got my note, and the necklace?'

'Ha! Well, of course, being the way I was at the

time, I thought your note was just crazy,' said Moll. 'I could barely remember either of you – because of what they did to me, you understand. And it all sounded – well, weird. I just threw the thing away. But that night I had a dream about the orchid necklace; I was in the storage cellar at school with you, Elsie, and we were making stuff, clothes and jewellery.'

'Yes, I remember,' said Elsie, helping herself to a couple of biscuits as she brought the plate over.

Moll accepted a cup of tea from Mum. 'I hadn't had such a vivid dream for ages, and it felt so much like a memory, and yet...it didn't fit! If it *was* a memory, then what was I doing mucking about in the cellar, making things...it just wasn't something Nice Proper Moll would ever do! It bugged me so much, I decided to get to the bottom of it. I pulled your letter out of the rubbish, and tried calling that number you gave. Some woman answered...Nolita? I asked for you, but she said you weren't available. I tried a couple more times, but I just got voicemail. Vijay said he couldn't get hold of Luke, either, but he didn't think anything of it. He said it happened all the time where you were staying – some out-of-the-way eco-hippy place...Kethly something?'

'Kethly Merwiden,' said Rorie.

'That's it,' said Moll. 'They're pretty cut off, it seems. Then Vijay told me what had happened with your mum and dad, which *he* knew about from Luke. He told me about the investigation, led by Inspector Dixon, and suggested we get in touch with him about it. But then we discovered someone had been eavesdropping on us...'

'Oh, that happens a lot at Poker Bute Hall,' observed Rorie.

'Right,' said Moll. 'Well, next thing I know, Vijay's lost his job, and I'm being sent to the Anger Management Centre for a "refresher course".'

'Oh, but Luke told us he wrecked it,' Elsie pointed out.

'That was him?' said Moll. 'Wow. We heard about that in assembly. Well, in any case, it didn't make any difference, just meant going further, to a different one. But as soon as they told me that, Rorie's note made sense to me, and I knew she was right – God, I feel so stupid!'

'Don't be ridiculous, Moll,' said Rorie. 'You rescued us! So go on; you got away somehow?'

'Yes. I played all sweet and compliant until Mrs Silk – your aunt – took me away. Then I pinched her Shel, and jumped out at the traffic lights. Straight away, I called Dixon.'

'Brilliant!' cried Elsie, clapping her hands.

Dixon joined them at the table. 'Under normal circumstances I'd have got straight onto her parents, of course,' he explained. 'But this was different. You two were missing at the time – Nolita as well. And I was in the middle of investigating that. Well, when Moll told me about this Poker Bute Hall "anger management" thing that she was escaping from, it...it was like that was the last piece of the jigsaw puzzle, joining up everything else that I hadn't found explanations for yet. So I couldn't call Moll's parents right away; they would just send her straight back to Poker Bute Hall.'

'How do you mean, it joined everything up?' asked Rorie.

Dixon took a slug of tea. 'OK, you know when you lifted the lid on the whole Minimerica thing?'

'Yes.'

'I was sure my team and I were going to lead an investigation. I couldn't believe it when we were told to hand over all the evidence, because a different team had been assigned to it.'

'Oh, no. Zedforce?' said Rorie.

'Yes,' said Dixon. 'This has been happening more and more lately and...well, now I know why.'

'No wonder Misty ended up walking free,' Rorie remarked bitterly.

'Anyway, the point is, it was out of my hands,' Dixon went on. 'So all your stories about what went on in Minimerica – the mind-manipulation and everything – remained nothing more than stories. But it was driving me crazy. I *knew* the Misty story wasn't a hoax – and the Minimerica stuff bore an eerie resemblance to that. But what could I prove? Nothing. That's where Moll came in. I knew there were problems with Poker Bute Hall, of course, but your uncle had already been locked up, I never thought there was any link between the school and the Misty and Nolita business, or Minimerica...until I got that frantic call from Moll about the brainwashing. Then it all fitted. And I remembered what you'd said to me, Rorie, about Poker Bute Hall being owned by a company...'

'Tramlawn,' said Rorie.

'Right, and that they in turn were owned by Rexco...I'm really sorry I didn't take you seriously at the time.'

'It's OK,' said Rorie. 'I probably sounded like a raving loony. But hang on, how did you know to come to Shenham?'

'Ah! Interesting: that arose out of pure chance, as it happens,' said Dixon. 'You see, I wanted to go out and get Moll right away, but I couldn't leave the station because the sergeant hadn't come in yet. Then he arrived, all breathless, apologising for his lateness, explaining that there had been a roadblock near Shenham. Well, what do you suppose sprang to my mind the moment I heard those words?'

'Oh boy,' said Rorie, looking over to Mum and Dad.

'Ah yes, the *roadblock*,' said Dad, his face like thunder as he recalled the way he and Mum had been abducted by Rexco.

'Exactly,' said Dixon. 'It all sounded only too familiar. Clearly, Rexco were up to something again, down at Shenham. I realised we had no time to lose. I commissioned the helicopter on the spot.'

'Thank God you did,' said Mum.

Dixon leant forward on the table, pressing his hands together. He fixed his gaze on Mum and Dad, took a deep breath, then paused momentarily. 'I can say this now,' he said in a low voice, 'up until then, we in the force were ninety-nine per cent sure you were dead.'

'Hey!' said Elsie indignantly. 'That's not what you told us!'

Mum stroked her arm. 'Well, he probably didn't want to upset you, love.'

'Of course,' said Dixon, turning to Elsie. 'Not while there was a chance, however remote, that your parents were still alive. I didn't even say anything after...well, the fact is, there was an announcement on the newsnet that they were dead, a few days after their disappearance.'

Everyone gasped.

'I just hoped you girls might not hear about it, since you didn't have access to the wider media at Poker Bute Hall,' Dixon added. 'Fortunately, I was right.'

'So what did they do, fake an accident?' asked Dad.

'Exactly. The official story was that Mr and Mrs Silk, in a hurry, ignored the diversion and went the tunnel route...and then, *pchoow*!'

'Oh!' cried Mum, suddenly shooting out of her seat in fury. She gave a sharp, humourless laugh. 'I'm not shockable any more!' she declared, thowing up her hands. 'I'm not!'

'Huh! There's no way I'd have burst through the barrier,' protested Dad. 'I may be impetuous, but I'm not an idiot!'

'No, of course you're not,' said Rorie. 'But what about that picture, Inspector? The one showing Dad's car speeding, close to the tunnel?'

'Well, I have a theory about that,' said Dixon. 'But first I want to know, Mr and Mrs Silk, what happened after you followed the diversion?'

Mum and Dad looked at each other. Then Mum said, 'We were flagged down…' She sighed loudly. 'By Zedforce officers. I remember thinking it odd that we were asked to get out of the car. But that's all; neither of us can remember any more after that.'

'OK, here's what I think happened,' said Dixon. 'When you got out of the car, they put you both under sedation simultaneously. Two officers, two injections. Then they took out all the things you were taking to Rexco – the inventions – and planted an electronic receiver in the car, so they could control it remotely…along with two dummies. Then they sent the car on its way, at high speed, into the tunnel. Flash! Off goes the speed camera, and with those dummies in the driver and passenger seats, it looks as if you're in the car. The camera was proved to be on that stretch of road between the roadblock and the tunnel. Car enters tunnel, and another remote device detonates a section of it. Then they dispose of the vehicle.'

'But you have no proof,' said Mum.

'No,' said Dixon. 'But Rexco did this; I have no

doubt about that now. It looked fishy all along! I wanted to see the vehicle and bodies for myself, but I couldn't get Zedforce to co-operate. They kept saying it was *their* investigation, and not my concern. Even my boss said the same thing. But until I saw the evidence for myself, I wouldn't give up.'

There was a knock at the door. A young officer entered. 'Sir, they really need you back at the station.'

'Yes, yes, of course,' said Dixon. He stood up and finished his tea.

'No, we're not done yet!' cried Rorie, jumping up. 'When are we going to know what's happening about Nolita and the others?'

Everyone looked at Dixon.

'All right,' he said, 'let me check in again now, see if there's any news.' Everyone waited while he contacted another squad member. He sighed heavily. 'Still waiting on clearance from our regional supervisor,' he said at last.

'What?' cried Rorie, about to explode.

'Darling, they're bound to be released soon,' said Mum, attempting to calm her. 'This story is going to change everything—'

'No!' cried Rorie, slamming her hand down on the kitchen table. 'That's what we thought about the Minimerica story, and look what happened! This is going to take force!'

Dad peered out of the window. 'She may have a point. I mean, if this is such a big story, where are all the reporters?'

Again, everyone turned to Dixon.

'But I don't have the authority to...no, damn it, you're right! The press haven't got onto this because Rexco have infiltrated them too. OK, how many people do you think you can round up?'

Chapter 29
Operation Tiger-lily

The large police van eased its way slowly up the steep hill. It was only three-thirty in the morning, but already the grey dawn was appearing in the east. Mum was in the driving seat – though she'd never driven such a vehicle before.

Elsie, for once, had been made to stay behind with Maya next door; this was too dangerous. It was dangerous for Rorie too, but she had persuaded Mum and Dad that she was needed. In fact, if she were truly honest with herself, what she really wanted was to disappear somewhere far away, just her and Elsie and Mum and Dad, and not have to worry about anything any more, ever. Well, maybe some day. But not now; there was unfinished business.

Mum drove on silently, preparing herself for the moment. Not far behind them were approximately six hundred other vehicles from different parts of the country, which had converged oh-so-quietly on the Welsh mountainside over the last four hours. For mile upon mile, Rorie had seen headlights winking at them as they progressed up into the hills; everyone was lying in wait, ready to pounce. One network message was all it had taken to mobilise such an army; there were an awful lot of people who were very shocked to hear what Rexco had done to their friends Arran and Laura Silk...

'OK, it's coming right up,' said Rorie, carefully scrutinising the glowing screen on the dashboard. There was very little on the satellite image to determine the location of the settlement; with their green roofs, all the buildings were well camouflaged. All she had to go on was the collection of cars and trailers surrounding them – all belonging to Zedforce.

Mum switched off the headlights and slowed right down. She drove on a few metres further, then stopped as soon as the barricade Zedforce had set up came into view. There was a sentry box on either side; Zedforce had ringfenced Kethly Merwiden, and were guarding it round the clock – and, Dixon strongly suspected, with guns. That was the scary part. 'The rest of them probably won't have guns,' he'd said. 'But who knows what other tricks they have up their sleeves?'

Mum picked up the simple, low-tech receiver the vehicle was equipped with (Rorie had reminded them that they wouldn't be able to use their Shels, because of poor reception). She spoke softly. 'Operation Tiger-lily ready to commence; over.'

A fuzzy, halting response told them that her message had been received.

'Oh-kaay,' breathed Mum, clearly trying not to show her nerves. 'Any minute now...'

Rorie couldn't make out much in the dark, but she knew what the drill was: Dad and Inspector Dixon had parked some way down the hill, then got out of the car and crept up through the undergrowth. They were to use tear gas again – which meant Dad and Dixon would be armed with respirators, like Moll had been during the Shenham raid. All had been acquired – unofficially, of course – from Dixon's police department. Rorie knew just how much Dixon was risking by going it alone like this, without authorisation; he would probably lose his job. How could she ever have dismissed him as no use?

'There they are!' Rorie announced in a loud

whisper, as she spotted movement up ahead. The shadowy figures merged with those of the guards. Rorie and Mum clutched each other's hands as they watched the struggle, so oddly silent from where they sat. For what felt like an eternity, but was in reality probably no more than about a minute, it was unclear who was winning.

Mum took a deep breath and gave Rorie's hand an extra squeeze. 'The longer that goes by and I *don't* hear a gunshot—'

'Oh, look!' gasped Rorie. 'There's Dad...see? He's beckoning us through!'

'Oh, thank *heavens*.' Mum floored the accelerator, and they shot forwards. The van zoomed into the central yard, causing much shrieking and honking from nearby chickens and geese. It came to a screeching halt, skidding sideways, all lights flashing and siren wailing.

They jumped out. 'This way!' cried Rorie, heading towards Lilith's house. Behind her, she could hear the commotion of many, many more vehicles arriving, doors slamming, feet pounding, voices shouting.

Meanwhile Zedforce officers were emerging from their trailers, blinking in their pyjamas. The gathering crowd made it hard for Rorie to find her bearings – but at least it provided some cover as they dodged their way through as best they could.

'Oh, where are we?' she cried, momentarily disoriented. Then, suddenly: a glimpse of Lilith, emerging from her house. Rorie grabbed Mum's hand. 'Over here!'

Lilith looked terrified. 'Rorie! What in God's name is going on?'

'It's OK,' Rorie assured her. 'Get Nolita and everyone – quick! We've got a van.'

'Oh, thank God – at last!' said Lilith. She ran back in. 'Come on, everyone, let's go – now! We're being rescued!'

Rorie and Mum followed her inside, and in no time the whole household had emerged. Nolita came forwards, looking frail and white.

'Mum, this is Nolita,' said Rorie, not quite believing it herself. The famous Nolita Newbuck – known to all as the world's most influential fashion maven – was barely recognisable without her sleek cherry-red hairstyle, crisp tailoring and power boots. 'Nolita, this is my mum! And my dad's here, too.'

Mum smiled at Nolita and offered her hand. 'Hi, I'm Laura.'

Nolita gazed at her, stunned. 'My God, it really is

you,' she breathed, apparently struck by her very strong resemblance to Rorie. 'I don't believe it! You got your parents back – this is a miracle!' She didn't shake hands; instead, she rushed forwards and gave Mum a big hug. When she withdrew, her eyes were glassy with tears. She sniffed loudly. 'OK!' she announced, switching abruptly into efficiency mode. 'Let's get the hell outta here!'

Rorie and Mum led the way, followed by Nolita, Lilith and Bilbo. Behind them, their clothing even more haphazard than usual, were John, Baby and Dream. Grover and Skye tried to calm their infant son as they ran; last of all, huffing and puffing, came Gula.

They were soon slowed down by the crowds; in no time at all, the whole central courtyard had become jam-packed with people. Many of them were rolling around in the dirt, fighting with Zedforce officers. The noise was deafening.

Rorie battled through the mayhem until suddenly, just as they reached the van, she froze.

'Come *on*, Rorie!' urged Mum, as they all began piling in. 'What are you waiting for?'

'I've got to go back for someone else.'

Mum turned to her, aghast. 'Someone else? No!

You're getting in the van – now!' She grabbed Rorie by the arm.

Rorie tugged away. 'No! I have to – it's someone who saved my life!'

'Do you see how many people we have on our side here?' yelled Mum. 'Someone will take whoever it is. Now *get in*.'

'*No*, Mum,' said Rorie. She yanked hard, and freed herself. 'I'm sorry...I'll be back!' She hurtled back through the crowd. *Idiot!* she reprimanded herself. Why on earth hadn't she gone straight to Luke and Pat's house? It wasn't far from Lilith's. And now...oh, no! Now they had probably come out to see what was going on – what if she couldn't find them? As she dodged this way and that through the throng, her mind bounced back and forth too: was Mum right? *Should* she just let someone else rescue them? Hadn't she already done enough? But somehow she just couldn't, not after what Luke had done. She needed to be sure that he and Pat were safe.

Rorie ducked and dived her way back. At least the sky was lightening now, making it a little easier to see. But the scene had turned into a full-scale riot. Rorie was by turns hauled along and thrown off-course; a couple of times, she was knocked right over. Then, as she neared the house, she spotted Luke, talking to someone. 'Hey, Luke, over here!' she cried, jumping up and waving frantically. 'Lu-u-uke!' But her voice was drowned in the commotion, and now he was moving away. The nearest house was wedge-shaped, and made of rugged stonework; she clambered up it, still calling...Luke turned, and—

Chapter 30
Shock

'You move a muscle, and you've had it,' said the familiar, gravelly voice. O'Brien.

Rorie felt something cold and hard jammed against her temple. Another gun? No, surely not. Wouldn't he have used it by now?

The whole shifting ocean of people gradually went into suspended animation, as more and more of them realised what had happened. They stood stock-still, gazing up in dismay.

Rorie closed her eyes. *No, no, no! Why* did she have to go and climb up like that, and make a target of herself? No, this was too cruel – just as she had Mum and Dad back!

'So, thought you'd come back, eh?' Rorie felt O'Brien's warm breath on her ear; her stomach churned. 'Clever move – I don't think!' He raised his voice to address the crowd. 'All right, everybody, listen up! Somehow you've all got it into your heads that there's some sort of conspiracy going on here…'

There were angry protests from the crowd. 'Let her go!' – 'Give up!' – 'You're done for!'

'Shut up!' yelled O'Brien. 'You lot are going to feel pretty stupid when you learn the truth. When you find out you've all been duped into some bizarre fantasy about Zedforce and Rexco. Shame on you! You should be a little more careful in establishing your facts…'

Cue loud groans of derision.

'All right!' shouted O'Brien. 'Let me explain! I am holding this girl because she is a criminal. But she is much more than that. You want to talk about conspiracies? *She's* part of the conspiracy. Yes! Her, and her parents…and there are others, too. They just want you to believe all this nonsense because *they* want to run things their own way. Her parents never disappeared, and she knows that!'

More loud protests.

'LET ME TELL YOU HOW I KNOW!' yelled O'Brien, quietening everyone again. 'Mr and Mrs Silk didn't disappear; they just assumed different identities. They did this – and bear with me, because I can prove it – by shapeshifting.' Amid the ensuing murmurings, he continued, 'Mr Silk is a scientist who has developed a way of changing his appearance completely, in a matter of seconds, merely by putting on someone else's clothing!'

Oh no! thought Rorie, suddenly realising where he was going with this: *she* would be the proof of his lies.

'Where on earth did you get that story from?' came a voice from the crowd: Dad. Poor Dad, who still didn't know about Rorie's powers of transformation.

'Let her go!' wailed another voice: Mum. 'Enough lies...let her *go*.'

O'Brien smirked. 'Well, they would deny it, wouldn't they? But they've been going undercover like this for some time, because they want to disrupt the carefully maintained harmony that reigns in our society today, and has taken years to build. Allow me to give you a little demonstration. Fergus?' A young Zedforce officer stepped forward and removed his jacket.

No, no! Rorie didn't know which she was more terrified of: the gun being held to her head, or the prospect of turning into Fergus – possibly permanently. The fact that he had severe acne was the least of her worries, considering that these might be the last minutes of her life, yet that mass of purple pustules just seemed to symbollise for her all the horrors of the situation. And Mum and Dad didn't know about her chameleon changes; what on earth would they make of this? It would be horrible for them!

'Put it on her,' commanded O'Brien. Fergus lifted the jacket around Rorie's shoulders...

'Aargh!' cried O'Brien, and all of a sudden the gun – yes, it really was a gun – was gone and he had loosened his grip on her. Rorie barely registered the presence of Luke, now engaged in a tousle with O'Brien, as she tumbled down the mossy roof and hit the ground with a thud. A Zedforce officer was right on her tail. As fast as she could, she scrambled into the bushes behind the house. Trembling and gibbering with fear now, she kept on going through the dense shrubbery, grunting as she elbowed her way through the dirt. *Got to get back to Mum and Dad...* But how, without being seen? Her mind was reeling; a fence appeared up ahead, and she thought, *Yes! If I get over that, I'll be free!* Then somehow she would get in touch. She reached for the fence, and—

A sharp, intense shock bolted through her entire being.

Every muscle tensed.

Let go, let go! She couldn't.

Nothingness.

*

'The poor love…it's the second time, you know,' someone was saying.

Bright lights. That smell – hospital smell. Antiseptic. Everything was…numb.

'The second time?' Not a voice Rorie recognised. A nurse?

'She's already been struck by lightning once, earlier this year,' explained Pat. 'Lord, but she's lucky to be alive!'

Gradually, the image of fuzzy figures came into focus.

'Hey, her eyes are open!' cried Elsie.

'Rorie?' The image of Mum and Dad crystallised before Rorie's eyes, their faces creased with worry. 'Oh, darling, are you all right?'

Rorie felt a chuckle bubble up inside her – she had no idea why. 'Yes…I think so. What happened?'

'There was an electric fence,' said Dad. 'Put there by Zedforce, of course. Oh, thank God you're all right!'

Rorie pulled herself up into a seating position. This was an awfully familiar sensation. 'I'm thirsty.' Mum held a glass to her lips and she drank, dribbling the water down her chin. Mum offered a tissue. 'Luke…' muttered Rorie, now remembering what had happened.

'Luke's fine,' said Pat. 'He's around somewhere...Luke!' she called. 'She's awake!'

Luke appeared. 'Hey!' He grabbed Rorie's hand and gave it a manful squeeze. 'You've got to stop this, y'know. You're gonna end up a walking power station!'

Rorie giggled some more, then hiccupped loudly. 'Oh no! Don't say – *hic!* – that!' She thumped her chest. She pictured Luke as she last saw him, struggling with O'Brien. 'But how did you do that? Sneak up on O'Brien, I mean? He had a whole team with him!'

Luke grinned. 'Ah, well! You know how them homes are built right into the hillside? Well, some of 'em's linked by tunnels, like the ones you went in. So happens, you picked one of the ones that was connected. All I had to do was get to one of the other houses, and go round. Then it was just a case of climbing up out of the skylight.'

'Listen to him being modest!' said Pat. 'You're a hero, my love!' She stroked his hair.

'Cor, those Zedforce guys didn't know what hit 'em with that posse of yours, did they?' added Luke. 'It was like the French Revolution or somethin'!'

'Word spread fast,' said Mum. 'Friends...friends of friends.'

Luke punched the air. 'Brilliant! People power!'

Elsie copied him. 'Yeah!' Then her face drooped into a sulk. '*I* shoulda been there. I wanted to fight in the relovution.'

Mum rolled her eyes. 'Thank God you weren't!'

'Right,' agreed Dad. He sighed loudly and gazed at Rorie. 'Bad enough as it was...oh, but if only we could have kept *you* safe!'

'It's not – *hic!* – your fault, Dad,' said Rorie. 'We'd have been fine if I hadn't stupidly gone and tried to be a heroine.'

'Don't say that!' said Dad. 'What you did was incredibly brave. Pat told us all about why you wanted to rescue her and Luke...'

'You *are* a heroine, love,' added Pat.

'Yes...just don't do it again, OK?' said Mum, her voice trembling. She blew her nose. 'But what on earth was that man going on about? Shapeshifting and all that! Is he insane?'

'Oh, well, see, what he was going to do was—' started Elsie.

'*Completely* insane!' Rorie butted in, shooting Elsie a fierce look. 'All the other – *hic!* – Zedforce guys were terrified of him, *weren't* they, Luke?'

Luke looked a little confused, but nodded. 'Uh,

yeah, he certainly sounded nuts to me…'

'But—' Elsie attempted again.

'*Hic!* Oh, these hiccups!' shrieked Rorie. 'Somebody'll have to give me a shock.'

'I think you've had enough of those,' quipped Dad.

'Food, then,' said Rorie. 'And a milkshake. I really want – *hic!* – a milkshake. And some sort of hiccup remedy. And a magazine, and a movie. Could you – *hic!* – sort that out for me?' she asked, gazing up sweetly at Mum and Dad.

'Sure!' said Dad. They turned to leave.

'Luke and Pat can help you,' suggested Rorie, grabbing Elsie's sleeve just as her little sister was about to follow them out of the room. 'Not you, Elsie,' she whispered. 'You stay here.'

The others left, and Rorie and Elsie were alone. 'Don't tell them about the whole – *hic!* – chameleon thing!' Rorie warned.

'Why not?' asked Elsie. 'They're gonna know anyway, aren't they?'

Rorie waved her hands around impatiently. 'No they won't! I mean – *hic!* – I don't know, maybe. But…look, I'm just not ready to go into all that right now, OK? So just keep quiet about it. For now, they can go on thinking Arthur Clarkson just died quietly at the pet kennels, like I told them. Remember? I really don't think they're ready for the truth.'

Elsie peered at Rorie. Then she leant over to get a closer look. 'That's funny.'

'What?'

'That mole – the Frances one? It's gone.'

Rorie leapt out of bed. 'Seriously?' She grabbed a mirror and held it up to her face. 'My God, you're right! Hey, it's gone, it's gone! I'm a hundred per cent Rorie Silk!'

'Maybe it was the shock that did it,' suggested Elsie.

'What shock?'

'The *electric* shock, silly!'

'Oh, my...' Rorie put down the mirror, and scanned the room. Spotting Pat's cardigan over the back of a chair, she grabbed it and put it on. Not for a moment did she hesitate; if she allowed herself to think about it, she might persuade herself it was too risky. Standing in the middle of the room with her arms outstretched, the baggy cardigan hanging limply over her shoulders, she waited, heart pounding. She ignored the dizziness she felt; that was just the effect of the electric shock. 'Well?' she asked.

Elsie drew nearer. 'Um...' She peered closely. She walked around her, looking up and down. 'Hmm.'

'What?' demanded Rorie, tense as a coiled spring.

'No, nothing,' said Elsie. 'I was just saying "hmm".'

'Well, say something else besides "hmm"! Do you see any changes?'

'Not yet.'

'Well, how long has it been?'

'I don't know,' said Elsie. 'How long does it usually take?'

'I don't know!' shrieked Rorie. 'I've never timed it! But it starts pretty much immediately.'

Elsie held the mirror up for Rorie. 'Well, take a look for yourself.'

Rorie stared hard at her reflection. 'Oh wow, this is incredible...I'm still me! A *hundred per cent me* – no Pat, no Frances... I'm free! It's all gone!'

'Hey, I tell you what else has gone,' said Elsie.

'What?'

'Your hiccups.'

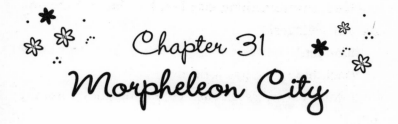

Chapter 31
Morpheleon City

'Minimerica', six months later

The stage was in complete darkness. The audience held their breath as one. Waiting in the wings, Rorie felt her pulse quicken. Now, at last, was the moment they'd all eagerly anticipated for so long. It felt like a lifetime...

Now a single spotlight fell on a solitary figure in the middle of the stage: Nolita Newbuck.

'Good evening, everybody.'

That was all she was able to say, before being drowned out by the ecstatic crowd.

'Yay!' cried Elsie, swept along by the mood. She jumped up and down next to Rorie, clapping her hands. And sitting in front of screens all over the world were millions more, eager to discover what had happened to Nolita Newbuck. Since her mysterious disappearance, there had been all manner of stories in the media:

Nolita Newbuck Struck By Mystery Illness

Newbuck Was Murdered

Nolita Spotted In South America

...And so on. Many of them were accompanied by grainy pictures or pieces of film, none of which, of course, were substantiated.

'I expect,' said Nolita – the cheers abated – 'you'll be wondering where I've been.' The crowd acknowledged this uproariously, then quickly quietened. Nolita gazed out at them solemnly. 'As you all know, the past six months have seen a massive change. A monster has been slain. This monster of a thousand arms had a stranglehold on every aspect of our society; from schools to industry, from the high street to the media and the celebrity machine. Its name was Rexco.'

Loud boos came from the audience.

'And at the centre of it all, like a spider trapping her

prey in her gigantic global web, was Tyra Spinorba...'
Nolita's voice was drowned out by a chorus of even
louder boos. 'With the help of her many avatars, she
was intent on keeping us all in an existence devoid of
original thought. And I, too, ladies and gentlemen,
was being held in the grip of that web. Yes!' She strode
forth, her voice growing louder. 'The Nolita Newbuck
you thought you knew, that doyenne of the fashion
world, was nothing more than a puppet, manipulated
to generate ever more and more demand for product.
And you!' – Nolita cast her pointed finger across the
audience – 'Every one of you here who slavishly
followed my advice...you too were victims of Rexco.

'And I am sorry. I'm sorry for leading you down
that path, and my message to you all today is: be
yourself! I was not myself. I was implanted with
a microchip and told what to do by one of the avatars.
But now, happily, we are entering a new era; one in
which Ms Spinorba no longer wields any power, and
will instead live out her days in isolation. Some of her
avatars, too, have been imprisoned; those who have
not actually committed any crimes are electronically
tagged, and will be watched very closely...'

At the mention of the avatars, Rorie pictured in her
mind's eye the army of them that had been coming for

her and her family just before their rescue at Shenham. She had thought about them often, wondering how much of their evil was down to conditioning, and how much was down to the fact that, genetically, they were identical to Tyra. Could they ever function as benign members of the human race? She had better hopes for members of Zedforce – though not for O'Brien. He was serving a prison sentence for extortion; this man had clearly been enjoying his role far too much. And now, at last, Rorie no longer felt as if there was an enemy around every corner, waiting to pounce...

Nolita, meanwhile, was moving on to happier things in her speech. 'I have something very exciting to unveil for you today,' she announced.

Elsie stepped forward. 'No, not yet, Else,' whispered Rorie, holding her back.

'Something that will help you to be yourselves,' Nolita went on, 'and which, most importantly, will revolutionise the way we manage the precious resources left to us on this planet. Ladies and gentlemen, please welcome the Silk family!'

'OK, now!' said Dad, and together they all went out onto the stage, in front of a huge screen that now pulsated with colour: first Rorie and Elsie, then Mum,

Dad...and Great-Grandma. All of them were dressed entirely in purest white.

The crowd went wild. Unlike the Nolita story, which had been completely under wraps, what had happened to poor Laura and Arran Silk had finally become headline news. By now, only someone who'd been living under a rock for the past year wouldn't know about the two brilliant designer-inventors who'd been secretly transformed into virtual robots, and whose memories had been so successfully erased that they didn't even know they had children; and about how they had been quite miraculously restored by their daughter, Rorie. Along with the siege of Kethly Merwiden, the scandal of the Silks had marked the beginning of the end for Rexco.

'Good evening, ladies and gentlemen,' said Dad. All colour left the screen, and now it too was purest white. 'As I'm sure you all know, when Laura and I visited Rexco back in March last year, it was to present our latest invention, which we understood Rexco were going to develop further with us, and take into production. And, as you know, that didn't happen. What has also been made public is the reason for Rexco's actions – that they were *afraid*. Afraid that everything that made them so rich and powerful was going to be taken away. Because they wanted to just keep on going the way they were, exploiting the people.' Dad paused for the loud calls of assent from the audience. 'What has *not* been made public is exactly what that invention was. It needed refining, it needed testing...most of all, it needed financial backing. Well, before we go ahead and show you our invention, I want to thank two very special people who have provided that backing: Nolita Newbuck, and my own grandmother, Lily Silk!'

Nolita joined hands with Great-Grandma, and the two of them came forward – Great-Grandma skilfully manipulating her automatic wheelchair – and bowed, to cheers. Great-Grandma raised her hand, and the audience quietened.

'Hello, everybody!' she croaked. 'It's wonderful to be here. And I mean that quite literally!' Everybody laughed. 'Well, now, he's jolly talented, my grandson, you know,' added Great-Grandma. 'And he's allowing me to do this, you know, intro thingy. So here goes: what you're about to see may look like science, but it is magic...oops, sorry, that should be the other way round. *Looks* like magic, *is* science. There. So, without further ado, Morpheleon Limited – that's us – present:

The Only Collection. So called because these are the *only* outfits you will ever need!'

First, Mum and Dad came forward. And, in much the same way as they'd done a year ago for Rorie and Elsie in their little basement laboratory, but with some refinements and the addition of some slick moves, they proceeded to explain the 'magic' that was happening before the audience's eyes – the colour-and-shape-changing of the clothing that every member of the Silk family was wearing.

Meanwhile, Rorie was in her element, parading around as the hem on her – now emerald-green – dress lengthened and broadened, as if by magic. Elsie held her left arm up and her right hip out, then switched to right arm up and left hip out and back again. With each flip, the pattern on her dress changed completely. Mum demonstrated the superbootshoes, which literally changed from shoes to boots as she walked. Great-Grandma twirled around in her chair, while the sequins on her beautiful evening dress went through all the colours of the rainbow. Dad removed his suit, to reveal a vest and joke underpants, and then shrank his suit and packed it away in a very small bag. The audience went wild.

'And now,' announced Mum, 'please welcome

some friends of ours – all modelling more variations of Morpheleon clothing!' On came Luke and Pat, Gula, Lilith and Bilbo. Each had reprogrammed their outfits from the Only collection to suit their own individual style.

Next came Artie and Tink, Nolita's old employees, whom Rorie had become friendly with during her days living with her. Newly hired by Morpheleon, they paraded on, proudly twirling in their colourful, ever-changing outfits.

'And now, please welcome a very special guest,' said Dad in a more sober tone. The lighting and the music became more subdued. 'Like us, she disappeared,' Dad went on. 'But in her case there was very little media coverage; just a small story ten years ago, quickly forgotten, about an "eccentric" technologist who, people said, had no doubt finally "gone round the bend". Her three-year-old child was taken into foster care, and the story just disappeared. Well, before she went missing, that technologist had been working for Rexco.'

There were hushed murmurings from the audience; the sense of shock filled the air. Dad went on to explain: 'We tracked her down with the help of the Chief of Police – then Inspector Dixon. He has been invaluable in helping us to expose this evil corporation for what it is. Like us, this woman had had her mind altered; like us, she didn't even know she had a child.' He paused; this was still not an easy thing to talk about. 'But now, following a comprehensive rehabilitation programme – which I'm glad to say has worked very well – she too is a part of our team at Morpheleon. Please welcome, newly reunited with her daughter Moll, Ansellia Campbell!'

Rorie looked into the wing, where Moll now emerged with her real mother, petite, and prematurely grey. Ansellia smiled nervously at the audience, but there was a sadness in her dark, deep-set eyes that Rorie knew could never be erased.

But Moll was clearly ecstatic – as was the audience. The applause went on and on.

They returned to the dressing room, where Arthur Clarkson was sitting waiting for them.

This was the *original* Arthur Clarkson, the one Rorie and Elsie's much-missed pet chameleon had been named after. He was a tall, stooped man with kind, shy eyes behind thick glasses. 'Brilliant show, well done everybody!' he said, patting each family member on the back as they returned.

'D'you think so?' said Dad.

Arthur popped open a bottle of champagne, and began pouring glasses. 'Great...just great.'

Elsie hugged his leg. 'You shoulda joined in, Arthur.'

'Oh, not me!'

'You know Arthur,' said Dad. 'It's a miracle we even got him out here.'

'It's true,' said Arthur. 'I'm glad you did, though. I'm most impressed! What a transformation, eh? Of Minimerica, I mean. OK, a toast.' He raised his champagne glass. 'Goodbye Minimerica; long live Morpheleon City!'

Everyone else grabbed a glass. 'Morpheleon City!'

Some of the wildlife parks and cityscapes remained, but 'Minimerica' was indeed transformed. The new Morpheleon City was still evolving. Now anchored just off the Welsh coast, it would be home to all of the company's manufacturing, as well as a museum where future generations would learn about the revolution that had been brought about by the Silk family.

'Well!' said Arthur. 'Do you want me to, um...?'

'Yes, now would be good,' said Mum, looking at Dad.

'Good for what?' asked Elsie.

'Well, I've brought along a surprise for you girls,' said Arthur. 'A present from your parents.' He moved aside, and only now did Rorie notice the domed object draped in red fabric on the dressing table. Arthur pulled away the cloth to reveal a cage; inside it was a chameleon.

Elsie gasped. 'Can we keep him?'

'Actually, it's a her,' said Mum. 'And yes, of course you can – that's the idea!'

'Oh, wow!' said Rorie. 'She looks just like Arthur Clarkson. I mean, the other one, of course...'

Arthur smiled. 'Of course.'

Rorie hugged Mum and Dad. 'Oh, thank you!' She reached into the cage and gently took out the chameleon.

Elsie leant over and stroked the creature's scaly back. 'So, what'll we call her?'

The chameleon was currently displaying a pattern of dark-red stripes on a gold background; it didn't take long for a name to pop into Rorie's head.

'Tiger-lily,' she said.

'Hey, yeah!' said Elsie. 'It suits her.'

'Perfect,' said Mum.

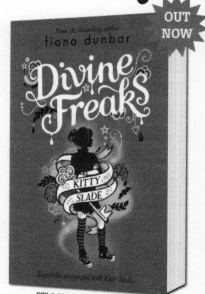

Here's a sneak peek of *Divine Freaks* . . .

People say a lot of stupid things about ghosts.

Let's face it, people do say dumb things about stuff they *think* they know about, but don't. And most people don't actually know the first thing about ghosts. How can I be so sure? Because I know quite a lot about ghosts – I see them all the time.

Number one stupid thing people say: they don't really exist, you know.

OK, just because *they* haven't seen them, doesn't mean they're not there.

Number two: they do exist, but only in old castles and stuff.

Wrong! They're everywhere – on the streets, in supermarkets…in schools. *Your* school, probably.

I haven't always seen ghosts. The first thirteen years of my life were a complete ghost-free zone.

Then things…changed.

Here's how it started.

I was in biology class, minding my own business, when all of a sudden this man appeared, about to murder a rat.

Not a nasty sewer rat or anything, but a lovely snowy white one, really cute. Poor thing was totally freaking out, waving its little pink paws about and gazing up with red beady eyes at this great shining scalpel blade about to slit it open.

The man – tall and hunched, with a mean grey face – just grinned hard. He was going to enjoy this.

Or he would have done, if I'd given him half a chance.

'Nooooo!' I cried, and ran over, sending my stool crashing to the ground. Mr Wesley was blocking my way so I had to shove him aside, which was a bit not-OK, really; he fell against the cabinet full of jars of random body parts in formaldehyde.

Rat-Man grinned his sickly grin, all sallow grey skin and yellow teeth, and then–

I lunged, but he wasn't there any more. I fell in a heap on the floor. He'd disappeared, along with the rat. *Poof!* Just like that. Gone.

'What in the name of…?' began Mr Wesley, as he

adjusted his glasses, his tie, his hair. The cabinet had survived, just.

The whole class was staring at me.

'I wanted to stop him…that man.'

'*What* man?'

Stifled giggles around the class, and I was thinking, what the hell's so funny about a creepy stranger suddenly appearing, wielding a scalpel? But Mr Wesley hadn't seen him…and neither, it seemed, had anyone else. They thought I was just mucking about – which, to be honest, I've been known to do when things have got like, really dull.

'There was a man,' I explained, getting up. 'He was just here! He was…' I gazed around: nothing. I blinked, rubbed my eyes.

Then all of a sudden he appeared again, this time in the corner of the room, by the door. 'There he is…over there!' I yelled.

Everyone turned to look.

He wasn't holding the rat this time. He just stood there, like he was ready to fend off an attacker or something. His vampire face was hard and violent now; the grin was gone. He held up his right hand, and in it glinted something shiny and sharp; the scalpel.

Don't miss the *Lulu Baker* trilogy!

The
Truth
Cookie

Discover a magical recipe book that gives Lulu Baker the power to change lives...

Lulu's dad has a new love, Varaminta le Bone. She's a sizzling sensation...and pure poison. How can Lulu make her dad see Varaminta, and her odious son Torquil, for who they really are?

Then Lulu stumbles into an odd little bookshop and Ambrosia May's mysterious recipe book falls at her feet. *The Apple Star,* together with some *very* unusual ingredients, might just do the trick...

Cupid
Cakes

Thanks to Lulu Baker and her magical recipe book, The Apple Star, romance is in the air!

Lulu and her best friend Frenchy are inspired by the school production of *A Midsummer Night's Dream* to play cupid to Lulu's dad and...Frenchy's mum!
But no sooner has Lulu whipped up the recipe for Cupid Cakes, and given Dad a taster – disaster strikes. Suddenly it seems like everyone is falling in love with the wrong person!

And something deeper and darker is worrying Lulu. Evil Varaminta le Bone and her tricksy son Torquil are back! Varaminta has uncovered the magical powers of *The Apple Star* and now she'll stop at nothing to get her hands on it...